"Federal agen
"Open the doo

"No!" The female voice yelled, "I know my rights."

Hailey banged on the door. "We just want to ask a few questions, Ms. Phelps. This won't take long and then you can go about your day."

"I'll go about my day when you leave me alone! This is police harassment!"

If Deirdre Phelps didn't want to open the door and talk, there wasn't much else she could do without probable cause and a warrant.

The neighbors probably loved the shouting match happening on their quiet little street, but this was pretty much the highlight of Hailey's day. There was a rush to her work, a satisfaction of being part of an organization that brought down the worst of the worst criminals and put them away. Justice. Honor. She breathed these things. Her heart beat by them.

Hailey heard the ratchet of a shotgun.

Eric launched himself at her just before the front door exploded.

Lisa Phillips is a British-born, tea-drinking, guitar-playing wife and mom of two. There's only one bunny rabbit now (sad face), but she's muddling through that. Lisa favors high-stakes stories of mayhem and disaster where you can find made-for-each-other love that always ends in happily-ever-after, and she understands that faith is a work-in-progress more exciting than any story she can dream up. To find out more, visit authorlisaphillips.com.

Books by Lisa Phillips

Love Inspired Suspense

Double Agent
Star Witness
Manhunt

Visit the Author Profile page at Harlequin.com.

Manhunt

Lisa Phillips

HARLEQUIN® LOVE INSPIRED® SUSPENSE

Recycling programs for this product may not exist in your area.

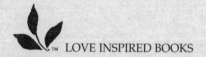

LOVE INSPIRED BOOKS

ISBN-13: 978-0-373-44653-7

Manhunt

www.Harlequin.com

Printed in U.S.A.

He sent from on high, he took me;
he drew me out of many waters.
–*Psalms* 18:16

To Scott. Thanks for putting up with endless questions about dams, boats, guns and computery-thingys.

ONE

The shackled man in the orange jumpsuit sat between US Marshal Hailey Shelder and her new partner. The SUV rumbled down the dark highway at two in the morning while rain pounded on the windshield. It had been raining for days, a torrent that left ranches and farms waterlogged and roadways covered with a sheet of water.

Hailey tapped her foot. The excess adrenaline of a prisoner transfer coursed white-hot in her veins, leaving her wide awake. But all she was doing was sitting in the backseat waiting for…nothing would be great. No activity at all. Just the routine movement of prisoner to airplane, and then they could go home.

Hailey should have been dead asleep in a food coma after her evening watching back-to-back cartoon movies with Kerry that they'd both seen a million times already—not to mention all that popcorn. But she wasn't going to skip her Friday night movie date with her twelve-year-old daughter, not even for a middle-of-the-night fugitive transfer. And definitely not when her ex-husband had Kerry every other weekend.

Half an hour out of town, the SUV pulled into the tiny airfield they used for covert, nighttime prisoner transfers. It was an out-of-the-way airport usually used for scenic

tours of central Oregon—tours that strategically circled
around the valley where the federal penitentiary was lo-
cated. The airport was only two buildings and the runway,
which was enough for them to make use of. The Marshals
Service didn't need the audience a bigger airport would
give them.

"I can't believe it's still pouring." Hailey's new partner,
Eric Hanning, leaned forward to look around the fugitive.
"What is with this state? Is it ever going to stop raining?"

Hailey couldn't stop the little flip of her heart every
time he turned those blue eyes in her direction. Even
though it was dark in the car, she could still picture them.
She shrugged, as if his presence was all the same to her.
Maybe if she pretended for long enough it would become
true. Besides, it wasn't like they got along.

"Maybe in a week or two." Hailey didn't want him getting his hopes up that the weather would clear. The rainfall
had exceeded record amounts days ago, but the Arizona
transplant didn't know that.

She and Eric had butted heads at every available oppor-
tunity since he'd joined the team. His insistence on learn-
ing and then implementing every nuance of procedure was
exhausting. At least the difference in their personalities
served to defuse whatever attraction was there.

Office lore said Eric Hanning had been transferred from
WITSEC. It must have been hard for him to go from something that cushy to a fugitive apprehension task force. But
she wasn't going to cut him any slack—that wasn't how
their world worked.

Hailey was the only woman on the eight-man team,
and she was finally not the rookie anymore. Eric Hanning
might shape up to be useless as a field marshal, but he was
at least good for getting her out of the lowest spot.

Truthfully, Eric was so good-looking she could barely

form sentences when his attention was on her—but she was trying to beat that, because those feelings had gotten her in trouble before. It didn't mean he was anything special, just that God had chosen to give him a face that could've been in movies.

And while Eric was probably a perfectly nice guy, Hailey was done with romantic relationships. Her ex-husband had soured her on even the idea of getting back into all that.

Deputy Marshal Jackson Parker, her coworker and tonight's driver, wound the vehicle between the office and the hangar. Yellow floodlights illuminated the corrugated walls of the building on her side. The prisoner shifted, and Hailey whipped her head back around to look at him. The last thing she wanted was any funny business. This needed to go smooth and easy, because she had every intention of getting home in time for Saturday-morning waffles.

Deputy Marshal Wyatt Ames sat in the front passenger seat. Both he and Parker were big guys, and it was squished enough in the backseat with the fugitive in the middle of Hailey and Eric.

The fugitive didn't move again. The shackles on his wrists and ankles didn't afford him much reach, but he'd still be able to do some damage in such close quarters. And Steve Farrell was notorious for the damage he could do.

His rap sheet was a lengthy list that included assault and murder, and he'd been found in possession of drugs and a stash of deadly weapons big enough to start a coup. He didn't discriminate either. Men, women and children had been left in his wake. In her estimation, he was about a millimeter south of pure scum, but soon he would be off to his permanent stay in the California federal prison system.

Visibility outside was six feet, barely. But a jet on the

runway would have been unmistakable. Hailey craned her neck and looked out each of the windows. "It's not here."

Eric lifted his watch so she could see the display. Who even wore a watch these days? Not that she could have gotten to her phone right now with all the gear she had on and the rifle she was holding. The illuminated screen on Eric's watch read 2:07 a.m., so they had another eight minutes until the plane was due.

Eric said, "I'm ready to get this done and get home."

Ames turned back to them from the front passenger seat. "Prisoner transfer cutting into your beauty sleep?"

Parker and Ames both laughed, though their humor had an edge to it, which wasn't surprising. None of them would totally relax until the prisoner was safely on the plane and out of their custody. Hailey didn't react. She knew what it felt like to be on the receiving end of their razzing.

Parker left the engine running and they waited. Five minutes later the radio on the dash crackled to life and the plane's pilot radioed in that they were two minutes out. Hailey heard the transmission echo in her earpiece.

Parker confirmed they were in place and ready. After he said, "Over," he nodded to Ames, who called the office on his cell phone and confirmed they were ready to begin the transfer.

Ames hung up the phone. "Green light."

"Let's get this show on the road." Parker accepted his rifle from Ames, who'd been holding both weapons.

"Seriously, that's the best you can come up with?" Ames asked. "'Let's get this show on the road?'"

Parker sneered. "Excuse me if my mental faculties are otherwise occupied."

"Yeah, it must be tough to have to concentrate on walking the orange jumpsuit from here, to down there." Ames pointed down the runway.

"Let's just go, okay?" Eric was apparently determined to be the voice of reason, but Hailey didn't mind.

She said, "Agreed. If we're going to get drenched anyway, then I'd rather get out now and get on with this."

Parker turned to them, his eyes on the prisoner. "Let's move."

They climbed out and walked to the runway as the four corners of a square, with Steve Farrell in the center. The downpour drowned out all sound except rain hitting the concrete and her jacket. In the distance, the airplane's lights came into view, high in the sky.

Rain poured off the sides of her helmet as Hailey scanned the area, keeping her senses open in case Farrell tried something. Her clothes had gained fifteen pounds of water that penetrated through to the tank top underneath. Even her socks were wet in her boots. When she took off her helmet later, her hair was going to be a giant red fuzz ball.

Out here in the middle of the night Hailey wasn't an individual, but part of a team made of four marshals guarding one fugitive. They had to get the man onto the airplane, and nothing else mattered beyond that, their most important objective. Any help they could call in was half an hour away.

"Go!" On Parker's command they speed-walked the prisoner to the runway. There was no hanging around. This wasn't about any of them. Except in the case of a debilitating injury, each marshal just had to do his or her job. It was a far cry from WITSEC, but getting his cover blown as an inspector for witness protection—by a reporter, no less…well, that hadn't been in the plan either.

Two months now. Two months of his life being upside

down. Two months of fugitive apprehension and prisoner transfers. Two months on a team with Hailey Shelder.

He'd denounced romantic relationships altogether after his fiancée had been paralyzed. Because while Eric would have stayed with Sarah forever, she'd pushed him away and refused to believe he still loved her. He'd tried to get her to listen, but eventually he'd been forced to face the fact she didn't want him anymore.

Eric risked a glance across the huddle as they strode to the plane. Hailey was all business, just one of the guys, dressed in the same bulky outfit they all wore. Her gun wasn't even trembling, not like the tiny shift of his. Wasn't she scared? His whole body was shaking, but if asked he'd have claimed it was the rain and the cold. Oregon seasons were killer to a guy who'd lived in Phoenix almost his whole adult life.

Parker yelled, "Let's go! Pick it up!"

They had to get Farrell on that plane.

Eric's earpiece crackled. A voice came on, male. The man instructed the pilot there was a problem and he shouldn't land. The wording was precise, using a code they only employed when there was an imminent threat.

The team shifted. The only one who didn't falter was Parker. "Hold."

The pilot radioed back. "Confirmed." The plane banked left and circled around, flying away from them.

"Huddle up." On Parker's order, they closed in and turned outward. Anyone who approached would have to face one of them, no matter what direction they were coming from.

Ames said, "What's going on? Who was that?"

Parker, the former SEAL, shouted over the pounding rain. "We're going back to the vehicle. On my—"

Something bright cut through the darkness, barreling through the air from the tree line.

Their SUV exploded.

Eric choked on his gasp. He could see Hailey was itching to run. The fugitive, Farrell, began to laugh.

They were cut off until someone could get there to assist them.

Eric scanned the darkness, but he saw nothing. Even with the light of the SUV engulfed in flames, there was no sign of the threat in the deluge of rain.

The fugitive bobbed from one foot to the other. His orange jumpsuit was drenched and his bulletproof vest was dripping, but he was still a beacon in the night. Someone out there had their eyes on the target. Whoever it was didn't want Farrell on that plane. But were they here to kill him, or help him escape?

A canister hit Eric's foot, and gas began to pour out in a cloud of smoke. "Gas!" Eric called out the warning, but they couldn't get to masks they didn't have. They couldn't even move from their positions.

Two more canisters were tossed at the edges of their huddle and more smoke chugged out of them. The cloud cut off what visibility they'd had and Eric's lungs protested the noxious smell of tear gas. How long could he hold his breath? Hailey coughed, and then Ames did, too. Parker looked like he was still breathing normally. What did they do to SEALs in their training?

Then there was nothing but smoke.

Parker yelled, "Hold!"

Deputy Marshal Ames hit the floor.

Something slammed into Eric's neck. It felt like a tiny rock. He tried to suck in a breath, but the floor swept up and hit him. Gunshots. Parker and Hailey both fell, too.

Eric touched the side of his neck and pulled his gloved

hand back, but there was no blood. He could barely breathe. It felt like the time he'd been winded playing paintball. The bruise had been on his sternum for weeks.

Beanbag rounds?

Booted feet crowded around them. He tried to move. The team was all down and the fugitive was laughing full out now, a sickening sound.

Steve Farrell stepped on Eric's stomach on the way over his body. Still laughing, he walked away. Their assailants looked like a swarm of cockroaches to Eric's blurred vision. He wiped away the tears streaming down his face— a product of the gas—and tried to focus.

The assault team was going to disappear into the darkness with an escaped fugitive.

Eric grasped about for his weapon, grabbed it and managed to aim at the man in orange.

One of his teammates fired.

Eric fired, too.

TWO

Just after nine on Friday morning, almost a week after Steve Farrell's escape, Hailey slumped into the back row of the briefing room beside Eric and handed him his coffee. The whiteboard at the front of the room was covered with pictures of Farrell, showcasing his life of crime over the last few years, along with his known associates. Beside it was a map marked with sightings of Farrell that had been called in to the tip line.

No one knew who had helped Farrell escape.

Jonah Rivers, their supervisor and the fugitive apprehension task force team lead, stood at the front of the room. They had another boss, Marshal Wilson Turner, an old-school marshal who oversaw the whole office, but Jonah was the hands-on man.

Jonah stood with his feet hip-width apart and his arms folded. "The blood found on the runway was sent off for testing. We still don't know who hit who, given both Marshal Shelder and Marshal Hanning fired their weapons."

Hailey's cheeks heated. Lying on the ground, thinking she'd been shot in the helmet, she'd realized she was unhurt and tried to do something to help the situation.

Beanbag rounds. Like suddenly it was important for them not to hurt anyone.

And apparently Eric had managed the same thing, because they'd both fired.

Too bad all she'd done was wing someone as they ran away. If she'd even hit the person at all. It could just as easily have been Eric.

Eric shifted beside her. She glanced over at his notebook, where he dutifully recorded everything Jonah was saying. He scratched above his ear with the lid of his pen. Maybe he wouldn't turn out like the rest of them. He did seem more studious than the rough-edged marshals in the room. That could be a good thing.

Eric shifted and pulled out his phone. The display said *Aaron*. He stopped the vibrating and slid the phone back in his pocket.

"Who was that?"

Eric looked up. "Huh?"

"The phone. Who's Aaron?"

"Oh, he's my brother."

Hailey studied Eric. There was no way that was all it had been. She knew for a fact her partner was keeping secrets, but for now, she'd let him be evasive. She couldn't imagine what it would be like to give up everything you had built, and move to a completely new city and start over. Still, WITSEC? That had to have been cool.

Her life had fallen apart in a different way when her marriage ended. She'd been tempted to get herself a new life, but around that time Kerry had been starting school and her dad's construction business was slowing down. Now he only took the odd handyman job to stay busy. It was just how things had worked out, but it meant Hailey had spent her whole life in this one county.

The marshal in front of Hailey raised his hand and said, "What about the rain?"

Jonah nodded. "They're expecting localized flooding

around the river, so the sheriff and the police chief are coordinating efforts to minimize the damage. The radar doesn't look good, though, and I honestly think the mayor's downplaying it. We'll see how it plays out and adjust accordingly. Rain or not, Farrell is still our target."

She tried not to flinch at Jonah's mention of the mayor, but it didn't help when two of the guys turned to smirk at her. So what? She and Charles had been divorced for seven years—whatever he was or wasn't doing in his mayoral duties had nothing to do with her.

She felt Eric's attention on her. "Something I should know?"

Hailey's cheeks warmed even more—a definite downside of having red hair and freckles. She turned to her partner. "Why would there be?"

His face said he didn't buy it, but she wasn't going to tell him all the details of her personal life if he wasn't going to do the same. They just weren't that type of partners, regardless of what most people thought of law enforcement. Hailey didn't bring her life to work. Not that the guys respected her need to keep her private life private. But that was a whole other set of problems, and she had enough to deal with.

Jonah said, "The clock is ticking. Let's get to work."

Eric's eyes were focused on her. She started to figure out how to explain, but her phone vibrated. She read the email and motioned from Eric to the door with a flick of her fingers. "Let's go."

He glanced up. "Where?"

"Jonah!" She was already walking away. "Hanning and I are out!"

Ten minutes later Hailey was driving through town with Eric beside her in her rusty nineties car. He frowned. "You missed the turn."

"No, I didn't. This isn't a latte run." His unrelenting insistence on following procedure was starting to affect her mood, like the rain clouds overhead that made everything dreary. "As for what this is, you'll have to trust me."

The country song on the radio was cut off by a loud buzz. An electronic voice said, "A severe weather alert is still in effect for all counties, including Franklin—"

Eric shut the radio off. "I might be new to the task force, but I'm pretty sure going off on a hunch is frowned upon."

Hailey pressed her lips together while the windshield wipers fought to quell the rainfall. "It's probably nothing."

"But it might be something?"

"You don't have to come." She shrugged. "You could get out at the next light and walk back to the office."

"And if something happens to you? I'll have to explain to the rest of the task force that I let you get hurt."

There was the crux of the situation. None of the good old boys on the task force wanted the little girl to get hurt. Apparently they'd overlooked the fact she was a trained marshal, just like them. She'd hardly have picked the toughest federal job—tracking down outstanding warrants, escaped prisoners and federal fugitives—if she was a wimp.

"All we're going to do is ask Deirdre Phelps if she has any idea where our escaped fugitive is." Hailey motioned to the backseat with a tilt of her head and made a right turn. "Check out the file yourself."

"What makes you think this Deirdre Phelps has anything to do with Farrell?"

Hailey hesitated for a minute, but if she was going to jump in then it might as well be with both feet.

After the debacle at the airport she'd been up all night reading and rereading Farrell's file. It had taken a week to track down his old girlfriend and confirm they were still in contact.

"Deirdre Phelps visited Steve Farrell every month when he was locked up in county for assault."

Eric flipped through the file. "Her name's not on the visitor's log."

"She used a fake ID. This morning I emailed her picture to a sheriff's deputy who worked at the jail back then. He just confirmed it was her."

"That was six years ago." Eric shook his head. "You didn't bring this to the team because…"

"You haven't lived in this part of Oregon long, so let me give you a crash course. Deirdre Phelps is the daughter of Thomas James Phelps the Third. He owns all four Chevy dealerships in the valley. She does not work. She lives in a condo in a gated community, drives a two-hundred-thousand-dollar car and spends her days shopping and getting manicures. She's practically royalty around here, and you do not mess with daddy's little girl."

"Still, couldn't you have just mentioned it to Jonah?"

"Fine." Hailey sighed. "Marshal Turner plays golf with Thomas James Phelps the Third."

Eric huffed out a breath. "Okay, I get it."

He should have, because Marshal Turner was technically their boss—Jonah's boss. Two years from retirement, his gut hung over his belt and he spent his days in the office looking at pictures of yachts.

"I just want to ask if she's seen or heard from her fugitive ex-boyfriend."

As of a week ago, instead of being transferred to his permanent federal vacation in California, Farrell was now back on the 15 Most Wanted list. And worse, his escape made her miss breakfast the next morning with her daughter.

The security guard at the community's gate frowned

at their badges, but let them in. Was he going to call ahead and warn Princess Phelps they were coming? Hailey couldn't do much about that, short of threatening him with her weapon. The security guard probably got paid more than she did, working in a neighborhood like this.

The streets were wide and free of cars, as if the residents had been threatened not to park there. The landscaping was immaculate, although waterlogged, since the rain was still falling steady. And yet, somehow not even a stray leaf was on the ground. It was eerie, unlike her homey neighborhood and the dated farmhouse she grew up in. Her roof leaked and the wind whistled through the upstairs hall, but at least her house wasn't sterile and void of humanity like this place.

Hailey popped the trunk on her Honda and reached for her two pairs of cuffs, the extra magazines for her weapon, and her flashlight. Eric's eyebrows rose under the bill of his government-issued baseball cap. *Go team.*

Hailey shook her head. "It's just a precaution." And more habit than necessity, even if it could be the difference between life and death. The extra supplies balanced out the professional weight of the star badge on her belt.

"I thought you weren't worried about this. It isn't a big thing, remember?"

Hailey rolled her eyes. Kerry liked to use that tone of voice when she needed to remind Hailey of something she'd said. It was like the kid was twelve going on twenty-five.

Eric's lips twitched.

Hailey frowned at him. "You're teasing me."

He shrugged off his jacket and snapped his belt on below his Kevlar vest. "Only a little."

"Must be a slow day."

He laughed. The yellowing bruise on his neck from the beanbag round did nothing to mar his looks.

They both pulled on black jackets with US MARSHALS stenciled on the back, and Eric followed her through the ridiculous little gate in the white picket fence of Deirdre Phelps's townhome.

Hailey unsnapped her gun and rested her hand on it. They were only there to ask Deirdre a few questions, but the possibility Farrell might be inside the residence couldn't be ignored.

The walk sloped up to the front door, while the drive curved down to the garage, tucked away below ground level like it needed to be out of sight.

Hailey ignored the bell and hammered on the front door. "This is the US Marshals, Ms. Phelps. We need to speak with you."

That would get the neighbors talking. Hailey would probably get into trouble for disturbing Princess Phelps's life, but she just knew there was a connection between Deirdre and Farrell.

She pounded again. "Open the door, Ms. Phelps!"

The voice that came from behind the door was muffled, but high-pitched. "Go away."

"Federal agents," Eric called out. "Open the door."

"No!" the female yelled. "I know my rights."

She glanced at Eric, and they shared a grin. Why did no one ever worry about Hailey's right to ask a simple question to someone who was clearly hiding something? That made her wonder again what secrets Eric was keeping, but there wasn't time for that now.

Not to mention the last thing she needed in her life was another man who was going to hide stuff from her. Not when she was trying to keep life as simple as possible for her and her daughter.

Hailey banged on the door. "We just want to ask a few questions, Ms. Phelps. This won't take long, and then you can go about your day."

"I'll go about my day when you leave me alone. This is police harassment!"

Hailey chuckled. "Open the door and tell me you don't know where Steven Farrell is and we'll be on our way."

"No."

Apparently Princess Phelps wasn't interested in taking the easy way out. Hailey only had her suspicions. If Deirdre didn't want to open the door and talk, there wasn't much else she could do without probable cause and a warrant.

The neighbors probably loved the shouting match happening on their quiet little street, but this was pretty much the highlight of Hailey's day. There was a rush to her work, a satisfaction in being part of an organization that brought down the worst of the worst criminals and put them away. Justice. Honor. She breathed these things. Her heart beat by them.

Hailey heard the ratchet of a shotgun.

Eric launched himself at her just before the front door exploded.

THREE

Raindrops hit Eric's face. He blinked up at the gray sky and shot to his feet, his weapon already in his hand. "I'll call it in."

"There's no time. He'll get away." Hailey hit the front step and Eric followed, their weapons angled down as they swept through the hall. Hailey probably wanted proof of Farrell's presence, or Deirdre's involvement, before they got reprimanded for going off on their own without informing anyone.

Eric hit the button on his Bluetooth and scanned the empty living room while he used voice dialing. "Duty phone."

He saw Hailey react, but she kept her eyes on the room as they swept through it, clearing the designer luxury of the first floor, room by room.

"Deputy Marshal Ames."

Eric didn't hesitate. He lead straight in with, "Shots fired." He gave the deputy marshal Deirdre's address. "Backup requested at same address."

"Farrell?"

"Possible location of escapee, but no sightings yet. House is not secure." Eric ended the call. Most women didn't pick a shotgun like that if they had the choice,

though it wasn't unheard of. He was guessing Farrell was
here somewhere.

The throaty rev of a muscle car preceded a crash. Eric
and Hailey both rushed to the front door. A black sports car
roared up the short drive from the basement garage onto
the street with a woman at the wheel. Where was Farrell?

"I'm guessing that was Deirdre."

Hailey nodded. "We need to finish clearing the house.
Then we can get a BOLO out on Deirdre. Farrell could
still be in here."

Eric followed her upstairs. The "be on the lookout"
order was already out for Farrell, but if Deirdre knew
where he was, finding her could be the quickest route to
the escaped fugitive.

And yet, Hailey still wanted to find the fugitive all by
herself. Of all the partners the task force could have assigned him, Eric was stuck with Hailey. She wasn't the
only marshal with something to prove, that was for sure.
But couldn't he have been paired up with someone who actually respected the rules? That must have been too much
to ask for.

It just proved how far Eric had fallen. With his rank of
inspector stripped, he was now a plain old deputy again,
demoted through no fault of his own. Clinging to the bottom rung, he got routinely stepped on by the more senior
members of the team on their way to the boss's fancy coffeemaker. He was stuck with what they all saw as the weak
link—the firecracker none of them had ever been able
to bring in line. Why couldn't she do what she was told?

Eric should have guessed when he saw her red hair. She
wore it tied back all the time, like she was trying to tame
her own nature, but little wisps of it always hung around
the sides of her face. He supposed some might call her
pretty, but he'd found her attitude eclipsed the understated

way she dressed. Maybe she should work on toning down her personality.

The front bedroom was clear, as was the bathroom. Two toothbrushes were on the counter by the sink and the toilet seat was up. Hailey entered the rear bedroom first. A mattress on the floor in the corner looked to have been used recently.

The floor was covered with papers, photos and reports. All of their personnel files. Everything Farrell's assault team needed to know about the four marshals who were supposed to have transferred him to that plane.

Hailey dug down and pulled out a map of the airfield. "They knew everything. Who we were, when we'd be there…all of it. Farrell has information on all of us."

Eric shook his head. "Why would he still need it now? I figured he'd split town first thing, but he's been staying here all week with this? Why?"

Hailey lifted a photo of a little girl and her whole body tightened. A picture of her daughter? The girl had Hailey's green eyes and red hair. He knew from the guys she had a child.

Eric set his hand on her shoulder. "Easy."

Hailey stepped away. "I'm fine."

Eric sighed. She was going to pretend finding that here didn't mean anything? "You're allowed to have a reaction, Hailey. Take a minute, and when you're good we'll get back to work."

"So I have a daughter. It doesn't mean I need any special concessions." She glanced out the window. "The team will be here in a minute. We should get downstairs."

Thunder rumbled across the sky, reverberating in his chest like a bass guitar cranked up to ten. The day had suddenly flipped from work to personal.

All he wanted was to punch in, do his job, and then

punch out at the end of the day. Not that going home to an
empty apartment and all the stuff he hadn't unpacked yet
was all that great, but Eric didn't much want to be chasing scum all day, running down outstanding warrants and
hauling in criminals like some glorified trash collector,
either.

The guys on the team thought they were so tough, going
after criminals on a daily basis. And the crazy part was
Hailey wanted to be exactly like them. As if being "one
of the guys" was something to aspire to. Witness protection hadn't just been a step up from this, career-wise—it
had been a calling, and he'd loved every minute of it. Eric
didn't want to live in the past, but it was hard when he'd
left behind so much.

Bye, bye dream job. Hello, hick town, Oregon.

He needed to succeed at fugitive apprehension, but he
wasn't going to sacrifice his heart and soul to do it. Not if
he could help it. Eric couldn't let it consume him the way
WITSEC had.

It was too risky, because if it went wrong, he'd end up
right back in those days after Sarah's accident, when she
didn't want to see him because she thought he couldn't
love her anymore just because she was paralyzed. So she'd
pushed him away, despite all his attempts to convince her
he still loved her. Eventually Eric had been forced to face
the fact she didn't want him anymore.

He couldn't let himself go there again. Not if he could
help it. He just had to keep everything compartmentalized.
Then there wouldn't be any risk of getting in too deep.

Find Farrell, and keep his feelings out of it.

Hailey heard the sirens before the stream of cars tore
around the corner onto Deirdre's street and pulled up outside the house.

Hailey took a deep breath and straightened her shoulders as the pack of marshals climbed out of their cars into the rain. Their jackets and ball caps dampened fast, and she could barely distinguish the patter of rain from the stomp of boots up the front walk.

"Farrell might have been staying here since he escaped. We're not sure."

Jonah actually looked impressed for a second, like maybe Hailey had done something of note. The forty-something's graying hair gave him a distinguished air, but she'd seen him cuff a four-hundred-pound biker without breaking a sweat.

The look of approval disappeared as fast as it had come when she told Jonah what they'd found.

"Not good." His eyes darkened. "Looks like Princess Phelps has some explaining to do."

Hailey nodded. This should have been a quick interview, a chance to bring new information to the team. Now someone—not Hailey—was going to have to tell Deirdre's father she was wanted for questioning. For harboring a dangerous fugitive, no less.

Hailey checked her watch. One hour until Kerry caught the bus home and went to her dad's for the weekend.

"Running late for something?"

She shot Parker a glance and scowled. "I'm focused. That's how I found all this."

Jonah stepped in front of her. "Parker, get upstairs and take a look."

Hailey smirked, but Jonah turned and caught the look on her face. "They're never going to warm to you if you don't play nice."

"It's been four years since I joined the team. I figure if it hasn't happened by now…"

Maybe their razzing her was their idea of respect. That was possible. But still, Hailey didn't like double standards.

"Besides, why do I have to be the one that's nice? Maybe they should go first."

Jonah sighed. "Why does my job feel more like babysitting than federal law enforcement? And I'm not just talking about the criminals."

Hailey opened her mouth, but Jonah lifted his hand, palm facing out. "Save it, Shelder. We'll get the techs to go through all this. Find out who Deirdre and Farrell were working with." Jonah folded his arms, his face completely neutral. "The BOLO will be updated to include Deirdre and her car. We'll take this from here. You two head back to the office."

Jonah wasn't going to ream her for going off unsupervised? "What's going on?"

"You want me to tell you that you did a good job?" Jonah asked.

"Might be nice."

"That's not going to happen. We all want to catch him, and you scored big with Deirdre and the files upstairs. Your actions versus the result, you barely broke even."

"What?" Hailey couldn't believe he thought she'd only done enough to outweigh her acting not exactly according to procedure. "But—"

"I get you want to catch Farrell, but this isn't the way to do it. One of these days this jumping the gun is going to get you in serious trouble."

Jonah ran a hand through his hair. "Once the team has finished processing the house we'll run through what they've found." He glanced at his watch. "How long until Kerry gets out of school?"

"You think Farrell's going to come after my daughter this fast?" Some of the other guys on the task force had wives, kids. Would they be targeted, too? "Maybe we should put a detail on all the families. Just to be safe."

Jonah folded his arms. "Look, we still don't know if Farrell was injured last week or not. It depends if he's already split town or if he's sticking around to pay us back."

"This is my lead, and it's Charles's weekend. Put someone on his house."

Jonah strode away down the hall.

"Come on, Hailey." Eric motioned to the front door.

Apparently Eric thought she'd done the wrong thing, too. "Fine. Let's go."

Together they stepped outside. The rain was falling in a steady stream. It felt like she was standing with her face against a sprinkler.

Hailey followed him to the curb, her drenched hair getting plastered to her head. "Jonah's going to take all the credit."

Eric looked back at her. Raindrops ran down his face. "You think?"

Hailey swiped the rain from her forehead. She should have grabbed a ball cap that morning. "Of course. That's the only explanation for why he wants us out of here. Haven't you learned anything? Jonah is going to make it look like I'm the victim and claim the lead for himself."

"But Farrell will be off the streets. Isn't that what we want?"

Hailey wanted to kick the gate. "That's not the point... or not the whole point."

"I thought our task force was a team."

"That might have been in the brochure and all, but guys like Jonah only know one thing. Being top dog."

Eric frowned. "Well, then, why do you stay if they treat you like this?"

"Why do you?"

"I'm trying to get my life back on track. And if you weren't so contrary, I'd ask if we could help each other out."

"Like allies?"

Eric's lips curled into a smile. "A peace treaty. What do you say?"

Hailey opened her mouth but didn't know what to say. No one had ever offered to stand with her before. She stood on the sidewalk with rain running into the collar of her jacket.

Why couldn't she say yes? It shouldn't be this difficult to accept a good offer from a fellow marshal. A marshal who had worked witness protection had to be trustworthy. Why shouldn't they have a true partnership?

His offer touched something that had lain dormant for so many years. She'd almost forgotten that place in her existed.

His anticipation seemed to fall away. "Forget it. Let's go."

FOUR

Eric poured two coffees and set one in front of Hailey. She tapped a brisk rhythm on the edge of her desk with her pen. He was disappointed she hadn't accepted his offer of partnership. Why couldn't she see how much more they could achieve if they simply combined their efforts instead of butting heads all the time?

He typed his password in and brought up Deirdre Phelps's cell phone records. She didn't have a landline, but she did have internet service. He wanted to get his hands on her computer, check what websites she or Farrell had been looking at. He'd always loved computer forensics, and now that it played a bigger role in his work, he could add to the short tally of good things in his life.

The office's double door beeped. A lanky man in an expensive suit pushed it open, and then shook out his umbrella on the entryway floor. His dark hair was shiny, either from the rain or from copious amounts of whatever he'd smeared in it to hold its expensive style.

Hailey lifted her head. "Great."

Eric rolled his chair toward her desk. "Who is that?"

"His name is Charles Turpin. He's the mayor."

The mayor looked at Hailey behind her desk, but didn't react the way people did when they saw someone they knew. Or someone they liked. Still, he came over, his Italian loafers clicking on the floor. "Hailey."

Hailey kept her eyes on her paper, her back rigid. "Social visit?"

Eric turned to his computer and clicked on the next page of phone numbers. The digits blurred together, so he rubbed his eyes. He probably should have remembered to bring his reading glasses with him to work, since staring at a screen for more than fifteen minutes gave him a headache.

The mayor said, "I have a meeting with Marshal Turner about preparations, in case there's any flooding over the next few days."

Hailey's eyes widened. "I thought the rain was dying down. It's supposed to get worse?"

Charles motioned to the door to Turner's office. "I should get to it."

She nodded. "Any plans this weekend?"

Eric's finger paused on his mouse. Were they dating? This Charles guy didn't seem like the kind of man Hailey would be interested in, but there was clearly something between them. It just didn't look like, whatever it was, was necessarily good.

Could this be her ex-husband? He'd heard through the grapevine that she was divorced from Kerry's father. But, this guy? He couldn't picture it. The mayor was way too suave, and Hailey was way too down-to-earth to fall for that.

"We're going to dinner at Milton's."

"The steak place?"

"Yes. Is there a problem?"

"Kerry's a vegetarian."

"Since when?"

Eric looked up and saw Hailey shrug. "I figured she'd

get sick of it after the first few weeks, but it's been going on a month now. You didn't know?"

"How am I supposed to know anything about that girl? She changes her mind as fast as the weather."

Eric glanced at the window. It'd been raining steady for days.

Hailey's exhale was controlled, like she was trying not to react. "Well, have a good weekend."

"Thank you, Hailey." Charles stepped away, but stopped. "Oh, I almost forgot. What with my meeting and all, I was going to have Beth-Ann pick up Kerry from the bus stop."

Hailey's entire body snapped taut at the name *Beth-Ann*.

"But Beth-Ann apparently has an appointment. You can get Kerry, can't you? Bring her by my place around seven."

"Charles." Hailey took a breath, like she was trying to rein in her frustration. Eric had never seen her act this way. "I'm in the middle of a case. I need to focus. There's an escaped federal fugitive out there who might be targeting us. And it's *your* weekend."

"I won't be able to get away," Charles said. Apparently unaffected, he strode off into Marshal Turner's office.

Hailey stared at the door, even after it had closed.

Eric wasn't sure which question to ask first. "I'm guessing it's complicated."

Hailey blinked and focused on him. When she saw he was amused, her eyes lit with a smile. "You don't know the half of it."

Eric chuckled. "Beth-Ann?"

Hailey rolled her eyes. "Charles's new wife."

Eric kept his expression straight. He had to handle this right or she would close off instead of opening up. "You and Charles were married?"

Her face shut down, as though she'd heard accusation in his voice. "Until seven years ago."

"Joint custody?" She nodded, but he didn't feel right leaving it at that. "Are you okay?"

Hailey studied him. "You're not going to interrogate me for all the juicy details?"

"I figure if you want me to know then you'll tell me."

Eric was more than curious about what caused a vibrant woman like Hailey to marry suave Mr. Mayor. They did not fit together at all, which might explain the divorce, especially with Charles being remarried. Had he cheated on Hailey? Eric was glad he hadn't been in town early enough to vote for the guy because he'd probably have volunteered to hand out flyers for his opponent.

No wonder she hadn't accepted Eric's partnership.

Hailey pulled open her top drawer and drew out a photo, which she handed to him. "That was a year ago."

An older man who'd bequeathed Hailey a wide jaw and his nose sat with Hailey and a red-haired girl around a restaurant table. The same girl Eric had seen in the picture at Deirdre's house. Hailey's daughter.

"How old is she?"

"Kerry will be thirteen next month."

Eric was thirty-two, which meant Hailey could easily be older than him, by at least a couple of years.

Her jaw flexed, and she answered his unspoken question. "I'm thirty-five."

Eric hesitated, measuring his words. "High school sweethearts?"

Hailey's face morphed into something that looked like pain. "We did get married because of Kerry, but we were in college. It wasn't long before I realized Charles was only pretending he wanted to be there. He loves Kerry in his own way. It's just me he wasn't able to live with."

"Did he cheat on you?"

Hailey brushed back a strand of hair that had fallen loose. "Let's just get back to work, okay?"

Eric shrugged like his world wasn't still spinning faster than normal. "Sure."

He knew she and Kerry lived with her dad. The guys on the team had told him that much about her when they'd warned him about his new partner. *Prickly* was the word they'd used. That had been an understatement. Getting her to open up even a little bit felt like a victory, one he wasn't going to take lightly.

No wonder she'd hesitated before, when he suggested they partner up. He hadn't even thought Hailey might be concerned about whether she could trust him or not. It made him want to prove himself, to tell her about his life and his own family so she would know for sure she could rely on him.

Eric studied her, and she didn't look away, so he turned in his chair to face her. "Thank you for sharing with me. You know I worked with WITSEC. That means I know a little something about keeping secrets. And finding someone you can trust with part of yourself is huge."

She waved away his words. "Whatever. It's not a big deal, Hanning."

Eric studied her as she got back to work. He knew she didn't mean it. Hailey seemed to live her life in "protection" mode, never letting anyone get close to her. Getting burned by her husband couldn't have been easy. Eric knew what it was like to lose a relationship with someone you cared about.

Had she loved Charles? If they'd had a baby together, she must have felt something for him. But it didn't necessarily mean they'd been head-over-heels in love. She'd avoided the question enough for him to know there was more to the story. Not that he cared, of course. But he was curious. And the more he learned about her, the more Eric wanted to know what was below the surface.

He looked back at the computer, and pain sparked behind his eyes. "Maybe we should get some dinner." The granola bar he kept in his desk had been stale, and now he was hungry again. "We could order pizza. You like pepperoni?"

She wrinkled her nose and shook her head. "Ham and pineapple."

Eric made a gagging noise and picked up the phone. "Two pizzas it is."

Half an hour later the door buzzed and the rest of the team swept in. Jonah wiped his mouth with a napkin and broke off to Turner's office. Two of the others had pizza boxes from the place he'd ordered them from. He should never have paid over the phone.

They tossed the boxes on the side of Eric's desk. A detective from Portland who'd been transferred to their team grinned. "Thanks for dinner."

Eric flipped the lid of the top box open. A single strand of cheese remained. He pushed up the other. The entire ham-and-pineapple pizza was untouched.

"Charles!"

Eric looked over. Jonah shook hands with the mayor, but it was more businesslike than personal. He couldn't tell if Jonah liked or disliked the mayor. Eric wasn't sure if that said more about Charles or about Jonah.

Marshal Turner hauled his girth out of his chair and slapped Charles on the back. All three men broke into a round of manly chuckles, though Jonah's laugh sounded more polite than anything else.

Eric sighed. The WITSEC office he'd worked in had been much smaller. Navigating the politics of a large fugitive apprehension team was proving to be a lot harder. It was going to take him a while to figure out each member of the team, and to ascertain how he fit into the group.

Eric slid out Hailey's pizza box and handed it to her.

She frowned. "You don't want any?"

"I'm not hungry."

Hailey's phone rang and she snapped it up. "Shelder." She listened. "Thank you."

She replaced the phone and looked at him. "Blood test has been done. They're emailing over the results."

She hopped up and strode to Turner's door, knocked and stuck her head in. Seconds later Jonah strode out. Eric got up and met their huddle around Hailey's desk, while she opened the email and scanned the test results.

"The blood found at the airport was degraded too much by rain and jet fuel. They weren't able to pull together a pure enough sample to run through the system."

Jonah's eyes were dark. "So we've got nothing?" He glanced at Eric for a second, and then back at Hailey. "Both of you fire a shot, one of you hits someone with enough accuracy to make them bleed, and it turns up nothing?"

Eric folded his arms. The bad weather wasn't their fault.

Hailey sat back in her chair. "We need another lead."

"We need to find Deirdre."

Hailey glanced at Eric and nodded. She'd done well earlier, coming up with the result they'd gained at Deirdre's house. Anything was better than nothing.

Jonah glanced at the window, where rain was pounding against the glass and gray clouds hung low in the sky. "Get back out there. Get me something on Farrell."

Eric nodded.

Hailey stood. "I have to pick up Kerry."

Jonah said, "Okay. Do what you gotta do and then get

back to work." He turned to Eric. "We need to know who helped Farrell."

Eric sat back down at his desk and watched Hailey pull on her jacket while Jonah strode back over to Turner's office and let himself in. None of them had expected the blood test results to turn up absolutely nothing.

His phone rang. The display said *Aaron.*

Eric sighed, not at all in the mood to speak with his twin brother. No matter how many times he was going to call.

FIVE

Hailey sat in the car looking up and down the sidewalk for Kerry and her neon backpack. Eric's disappointment in her refusing his offer of a partnership stung. Still, something kept Hailey on the ledge instead of jumping off and trusting Eric completely. She just didn't want to admit to herself that it had everything to do with Charles.

Eventually the team was going to see her for the asset she was. Eric was a decent partner, but he didn't get what she was trying to do. He had no need to prove himself to anyone, but Hailey had to keep the doubts at bay. She couldn't let herself be ruled by what the people in this town had thought of her for so long.

Kerry needed to grow up knowing her mom fought for what she wanted. She needed to know what strength was and be able to call on it herself. Kids learned by example, and Hailey intended her life to show how far she could still go, in spite of the bad choices she'd made in her teen and college years. It was that or curl up and cry, and weakness was no good.

She called Charles.

"Yes?"

Did he have to say it like that? "Kerry isn't here. Beth-Ann didn't get her after all, did she?"

"I told you she has an appointment. Kerry isn't in the cul-de-sac?"

"What cul-de-sac? I'm at the bus stop." She shifted in her seat and peered out the windshield. There was a street a ways up—was that what he was talking about? And why couldn't he have told her that in the first place?

He sighed. "Kerry waits to be picked up in the cul-de-sac."

And if she didn't know Hailey was the one picking her up, Kerry was probably waiting there. "North of the bus stop?" She got out and started walking, squinting to read the road sign. "Almera?"

"Yes." He hung up.

Hailey shoved her phone in the back pocket of her jeans. She rounded the corner and saw a dark-colored muscle car stopped in the middle of the street at an angle. The driver's door was open, and the dome light was on.

Farrell had a grip on Kerry's arm, and was pulling her toward the car. Kerry was kicking at his legs, tugging on him and valiantly trying to dislodge his hold on her. *That's my girl.*

"Hey!" Hailey drew her weapon as she ran. "Let her go, Farrell."

Kerry's whole body jerked and she looked over. "Mom!"

Hailey aimed her weapon at the escapee, her pounding pace bringing her closer to them. "Hands on your head, Farrell."

His eyes narrowed when he saw how close she was. Had he been so focused on taking Hailey's daughter he hadn't registered her approach?

He let Kerry go and ran for the car door. Kerry yelped and hit the ground, landing in a sprawl on top of her backpack, which was still on her back.

Farrell pulled away, swinging the car around. The door slammed as he drove away.

Hailey knelt by Kerry. "Are you okay?"

"Yeah, Mom." She smiled, but Hailey saw her lip quiver. "Thanks for not being late."

Hailey hauled her daughter to her feet and wrapped her arms around her. She gave Kerry a quick squeeze before she leaned back, pulling out her phone. "One second, okay?"

Kerry saw the cell phone and nodded, burrowing into Hailey's coat.

Hailey looked down at her while the phone rang. "Where's your jacket? You're soaked."

Kerry shrugged. "I was too hot."

On the other end of the line, Jonah picked up. "Rivers."

"Farrell just tried to abduct Kerry."

It took ten minutes for them to reach the cul-de-sac, at which point Hailey and Kerry were both soaked, though she'd made Kerry get out the jacket from her backpack and actually put it on.

Jonah's gaze scanned Kerry as he walked over. "Both of you okay?"

Hailey nodded under the umbrella she'd retrieved from her trunk, and Kerry moved closer to her. The passel of big men all making their way over was likely an imposing sight.

She turned Kerry away from them, and said, "Tell me what happened."

Kerry took a deep breath. "I got off the bus with Sara, but Beth-Ann always waits in the cul-de-sac. When I walked around the corner she wasn't there yet. So I waited."

Hailey's stomach was so tight it hurt. She shouldn't have eaten that pizza.

"I was texting you to say bye, because I knew I wouldn't see you until after school on Monday. I heard a car pull up, and I thought it was Beth-Ann. This big dude was getting out. He looked like Carissa's dad."

That meant he had long, dirty blond hair. Like Farrell. Jonah caught her gaze and mouthed, *Farrell?*

Hailey nodded and looked back at Kerry. "What happened then?"

"I backed up, but he grabbed me. So I screamed as loud as I could. And then I did that thing you showed me, and I stomped his foot. I think it worked because I have my boots on. He yelped, and I yanked my arm hard and then I saw you and he let go of me." Kerry took a deep breath.

"Did he say anything?"

Kerry shook her head, her cheeks flushed.

Hailey knew her daughter's instincts were sharp, because she'd made sure they were that way. Kerry didn't need to live in a bubble in which the world was a safe place. That was a lie. She needed to be able to take care of herself.

And this proved it.

A Mercedes pulled around the corner, braking suddenly right in front of them. Charles parked and jumped from the car.

"Daddy!"

Kerry shoved the umbrella at Hailey and flew to him, burying herself in his chest. Charles patted her head and looked at Hailey. "What's this about your escaped fugitive almost kidnapping my daughter?"

My daughter. Not *our* daughter. Hailey didn't have time to get into that with him, so she let it go. "It's true."

She wasn't going to lie. Charles needed to be concerned. Hailey wanted him on high alert when it came to watching out for Kerry this weekend, not assuming the danger was over, since the guy got away.

Maybe she could get her dad to stay at a hotel for a few days as well.

Hailey sighed, realizing she needed to let Kerry go with Charles. She turned to Jonah. "Do we need Kerry any longer, or can she get out of the rain?"

"She can go."

Hailey looked at Charles. "Why don't you get her settled at your house?"

Kerry turned back from the embrace with her dad and looked at Hailey.

"I'll call you later, okay?"

Kerry nodded and sniffed, pulling away from her father. Hailey put her hand on Kerry's cheek. "You did great." She wiped her daughter's tears with her thumbs and then kissed her forehead. "Love you."

"Love you too, Mom."

Charles looked down his nose at Hailey. "We're going to be talking about this."

Hailey smiled sweetly. "I'll look forward to that."

She watched Kerry go with Charles. It was like having her heart ripped out, every single time. Gifting someone she didn't totally trust with everything that was valuable to her and trying to be okay with it.

She could do a drive-by check of their house later, and Kerry had the cell phone Charles had given her for Christmas. It wasn't like Hailey would be out of the loop. But tell her heart that.

Jonah yelled, "Parker. Ames. You're on protection detail." He turned back to her and Eric, folding his arms again. She'd decided a while back it was his default thinking pose. "What is your read on this situation?"

Hailey took a breath. "I just don't know why he would pick Kerry, of all people. Is he trying to get to me? Surely there's someone better on the team. Or is this because he saw me at Deirdre's?" She shrugged. "I have no idea."

Hailey was shaking, the aftereffects of what had just happened. She gripped the umbrella handle tighter.

Standing beside Jonah, Eric's frame was dwarfed by their boss's. "You taught her self-defense?"

"Yes." Hailey frowned at him. Didn't every parent do that? His eyebrows twitched. "She has to be able to protect herself."

Eric lifted his hands. "Hey, I'm not saying it's a bad thing at all. Not if it potentially saved her life."

His words penetrated her heart, and Hailey's stomach turned over. Her hands shook more, and sweat broke out along her hairline.

Eric's face flashed with worry. "Hailey—"

Jonah stepped forward until his head was almost under the umbrella. "Take a deep breath. It'll pass."

Hailey waited through the surge of nausea, and then whispered, "He could have killed her. He could have taken her, and—"

Jonah said, "You gave her the skills to defend herself, and she did."

Hailey nodded.

Jonah put his hand on her shoulder. "This won't be the last time it hits you, but you just have to roll with it. You're stronger than the fear. And smarter."

Hailey stared at him, shocked that he seemed to know what he was talking about. And he'd actually complimented her. "I'm okay."

Eric stepped closer. "I'm sorry. I'm glad she's fine and that you were here. Kerry seems like a really level-headed kid. And if that's down to you in part, then you must be a pretty great mom."

Hailey didn't know what to do with all the sweetness coming at her. These were supposed to be macho guys who took down fugitives and then grabbed the file for the next one and got to work. "All right, enough of the mushy stuff."

Neither of them looked convinced that she wasn't brushing off their concern just because she was uncomfortable. But they still let her do it.

Jonah's phone rang. He stepped aside and spoke in a low tone.

Eric studied Hailey's face, rain dripping off the front of his ball cap. "Are you really okay?"

"Of course not. My child nearly got abducted."

"Are you going to be able to work this case? Jonah will probably let you work from the office until Farrell is found. It might be good for you to be out of the loop from now on."

Hailey's eyes narrowed. "Because Farrell thinks he can try to take my child? I don't think so, Hanning. I'm not sitting this one out, no way. Just try and stop me from running this guy down and putting him away."

"Good." Eric nodded. "Anything you need, you just tell me."

"Just like that?"

"Why not?"

Hailey didn't know why not. No one had ever offered her unconditional assistance before. What was with this guy? They didn't make men like this anymore. Maybe they all lived in Phoenix and never came north unless they were transferred for work, like Eric had been.

There was no other explanation. He had to have an ulterior motive. She just didn't know what it was yet.

"What are you thinking about?"

Hailey jerked free from her thoughts. "Nothing."

Eric's lips curled up. "Sure it was."

Hailey shook her head. "Who *are* you?"

Jonah strode back over. "Deirdre Phelps was marched into the marshal's office by her father and his lawyer. She is prepared to answer our questions."

SIX

Jonah said, "You want to do the interview, since it was your lead?"

Hailey couldn't believe it. He wanted to give her the credit now?

Eric shifted and pinched her finger behind his back. "Yes, she does."

Jonah walked to his vehicle. Hailey glanced at Eric and mouthed, *What is going on?* A smile stretched his lips, and he shrugged.

There must be something in the water, because the two of them were acting crazy. Jonah was giving her actual responsibility, and Eric was insisting he help her, with no strings attached. This whole week had been beyond bizarre. When she woke up tomorrow, maybe they would all be back to their usual prickly selves.

The car sprayed up water the whole way back to the office. Eric couldn't imagine what Hailey was going through. Once upon a time he'd thought he would end up married with children of his own.

Sarah's injury had killed whatever love existed between them when she couldn't accept that Eric loved her even though she was paralyzed. Now he couldn't see sharing his life with anyone, or living life as part of a couple instead of as his own man. He was far too set in his ways.

Eric glanced over at her, his fingers gripping the steering wheel. He had no frame of reference for the fear written on her face. His brother and Mackenzie, his brother's wife, were his family. But they were capable adults who had seen their share of trouble and pulled through it together.

Hailey might need someone to partner with her so she could keep her focus, but apparently she didn't want that person to be him. Eric had already offered to help her twice, and she'd turned him down both times. He wasn't about to make the offer again, not when the rejection still stung. They could work together as part of the team, but if they were going to be true partners she had to be the one to bring it up next time.

Hailey entered the conference room, her clothes still damp, but with a fresh cup of coffee. Deirdre's father was in the room, his stern eyes on his daughter. His hair was dyed dark brown, but his eyebrows and the chest hair in his open collar were mostly gray. He had a fake tan and gold rings on both hands. Thomas James Phelps the Third might have been a millionaire, but he was still a car salesman.

The lawyer looked old money. He seemed completely disinterested in the family drama going on.

Hailey set her cup on the table and sat. She gave Deirdre a small smile and tried something she'd never had occasion to use yet in her job. She cocked her head to the side. "Mrs. Henley's English Lit class." She pointed to the stunned woman across the table and smiled. "Back row, next to Gemma Malone."

Deirdre blinked. "Who...?"

"Hailey Shelder. Front row, closest to the window."

"No way!"

Hailey laughed. "Yeah, it's not something I enjoy re-living."

Deirdre laughed, but hesitantly, as if she wasn't sure she was supposed to. "I'm sure. I remember the hair."

Hailey had learned with time to tame her big red hair. "It was definitely memorable." They shared a laugh. When the moment died down, Hailey said, "I don't remember Farrell, though."

Deirdre's smile dropped. "He didn't go to school with us. He was older."

"And you stayed friends all these years?"

"I wouldn't say friends." Deirdre swallowed, like there was a bad taste in her mouth. There was also an indecipher-able look in her eyes Hailey couldn't figure out. "He takes what he wants. He doesn't care about anyone but himself."

Hailey nodded. "How long has he been staying at your house?"

The lawyer raised his hand. He leaned in and spoke in Deirdre's ear.

The woman nodded. "I just want to help you find him, to do my part as a concerned citizen."

"Very well." There wasn't much else Hailey could say, not when Deirdre was here of her own volition. "Where can we find him?"

Deirdre squeezed her fingers together on the table. "He said something about getting his own. I figured he was talking nonsense, but it was like he really believed he was onto something."

"Is he waiting for something? Or looking?"

"I think he's still looking, which is why he said he couldn't split town, because he's not ready. Like he's not sure where it's at, whatever it is." Deirdre ran a shaky hand through her hair, which was as perfect as it had been in high school. "But whatever it is, it's the reason he escaped."

"Did you give him anything, or do anything, or go anywhere because he asked you to?"

"No, he just asked a bunch of questions about going online and searching old newspapers and such. I told him to go to the library. I don't know how to do that stuff."

"What about the files in your house?" Hailey studied her. "What can you tell me about that?"

Deirdre shook her head. "I had no idea that was even there. He kept that door locked and didn't tell me anything about it. I just want to forget all this happened. Please, catch him. You don't know what he's like."

"Who helped him escape?"

"I don't know."

"You didn't help them?"

The lawyer shifted in his seat. Deirdre glanced at him and then said, "Steve just called me last weekend. I didn't even know what was going on until I saw it on the news."

"So you don't know why Farrell had files on US marshals in your house? Private information."

"No!"

"You realize this makes you an accomplice, right?"

Deirdre's eyes widened. "I'm trying to help you."

"So tell me what Farrell wants."

"It's nothing. He's just looking for some jewelry or something. Stolen stuff from years ago. I don't know anything else."

Stolen jewelry?

Everything Hailey knew about unsolved thefts flipped through her mind like entries in a rolodex.

She grabbed her coffee and stood. "Thank you for your time, Ms. Phelps."

* * *

Eric ran his hands down his face. Deirdre's phone records were a lesson in too much money, too little responsibility. Her credit card statements were nauseating.

"Anything?"

Eric looked up. Jonah was beside his desk with the assessing look he got when he was testing you.

Eric said, "Phone records were a bust. I can't help wondering about this stash Farrell is after, and what he wants from Kerry. If he had a hand in the original theft, then it could be an old score he never claimed. That would mean it's been sitting for years, which is unlikely, but not impossible."

Hailey was on the far side of the office at the coffee pot, pouring herself a cup. She had her thinking face on. He hoped she didn't burn herself by accident.

Eric continued, "That also means we now have more accomplices to identify. Known associates, family and extended family members he might still have contact with."

"Course of action?"

"Go back further. Look into possible associates and any heists they might have done. Scores which could've pulled in a haul big enough that he still wants to get his hands on it, even years later. Unsolved robberies, that kind of thing. Though, why he's doing this now bothers me. And what it has to do with Hailey and her daughter."

"So figure it out."

"Figure what out?" Hailey strode over, confident and graceful on her heels.

Eric shook his head. "Just talking about the case. How are you doing?"

Hailey sat, her face lacking expression. "I'm fine."

Sure she was. Hailey might like to act tough, but he'd seen her checking her phone every thirty seconds since they left the police station, and typing furiously on it several times—replying to texts from Kerry, probably.

Jonah rapped his knuckles on the edge of the table. "Let me know what you come up with."

Eric glanced at the window. The twilight sky was nearly black from the low clouds and the steady patter of rain. "It's looking bad out there."

"I guess." Hailey squinted at the darkness outside. "Maybe Charles was right about flooding. I hope not. It won't make catching Farrell any easier."

"Have you worked a flood before?"

Hailey shook her head. "The last time there was a bad flood I was in junior high. The whole town was evacuated. Our house didn't get damaged, because it's on the top of a hill, and my dad decided it should be a safe zone."

"Like a place for evacuees to go?"

She nodded, her eyes distant. "My mom was up for two days straight making coffee, getting more blankets and cooking for everyone. She passed away six months later. She had cancer."

Eric winced. "I'm sorry for your loss."

"It was a long time ago."

Hailey turned to her work, so Eric did the same. Sitting there wasn't going to accomplish much. Not if he didn't look at the big picture, the efforts of the entire team.

The clock was ticking on their escapee. Days would soon turn into weeks, and the trail had been almost cold before Hailey discovered the Deirdre Phelps angle. He couldn't deny she had a knack for this. But now the case had cracked open, and what had come out made about as much sense as Hailey's pineapple on her pizza.

If this went on much longer, the likelihood of Farrell seriously hurting someone in pursuit of what he wanted would increase. They couldn't risk losing Farrell forever. US marshals didn't let that happen.

The team had been given a free pass with the abduction attempt on Kerry, but the longer Farrell was free, the more likely it was that he would try again—or turn his attention elsewhere. Another victim might not be as clear-headed as Kerry.

Eric felt a surge in his chest—care that he wasn't sure was about Kerry or Hailey. He wanted to protect them both. If Farrell was targeting Hailey's daughter, then Eric was going to do everything in his power to help them stay safe until the escapee was back behind bars.

"Are you okay?"

Eric looked up. Hailey's head was tilted to the side and her brow was crinkled. He shrugged one shoulder. "I was just thinking."

"Must have been pretty deep. Who knew?"

Eric felt his mouth expand into a smile. She had a whole lot to learn if she thought he was just another federal agent, all brawn and no brains. He tapped his mouse and a picture came up. "Bingo."

Hailey got up and came over. "What do you have?"

"A picture of Farrell from his high school yearbook— not that he ever graduated. I figured it might come in handy for finding who his friends were and seeing what he was up to."

Hailey gasped.

"What?"

"That's..." She sputtered. "Farrell is..."

"Hailey. What?"

"He was one of Charles's friends."

SEVEN

Water sprayed up from the tires as Eric sped through town. Hailey sat in the passenger seat, making call after call, trying to get Charles or Beth-Ann on the phone, but with no response. She hit a slew of buttons again and put the phone to her ear.

"Come on. Answer the phone."

She jabbed the screen on her phone and cried out in frustration.

"Nothing?"

"Voice mail. Parker and Ames are supposed to be protecting her. They better have an explanation for this."

"Maybe the weather is affecting their phones?"

Hailey shot him a look. "You don't really believe that, do you?"

Eric didn't, but what other explanation could there be? Parker and Ames were solid guys, good marshals. At least so far as Eric had seen since he'd joined the team. If they'd been incapacitated by Farrell this time—even though they'd be on alert after what happened at the airport—that would take things to a whole new level. For Farrell, and for the team.

Eric pulled over where Hailey indicated, in a gated neighborhood much like Deirdre Phelps's. This one was full of two-story houses that screamed money. An SUV with government plates was parked at the curb out front.

The passenger door was wide open, the inside light on.

Eric drew his weapon as they approached. The rain was hammering down now, destroying his ability to hear anything or to anticipate anyone coming up behind him. He scanned the area as Hailey did the same.

Ames hung out of the vehicle's door, his head on the sidewalk, feet still tucked at an awkward angle inside the vehicle. Eric scanned the area and pressed two fingers to the underside of Ames's neck. His pulse was faint and slow.

Hailey yelled over the noise of the rain. "I'm going up to the house."

Eric nodded. "I'll call this in and find Parker." He pulled out his phone and called for an ambulance and for police presence before he hung up and called Jonah to report what had happened.

"Parker already called it in. He's with Kerry. You find Farrell."

"Yes, sir."

"I'll be there in ten."

Minutes later an ambulance pulled around the corner. Eric waited until the EMTs came over with all their gear, and then circled the house looking for Parker…and Farrell.

Both the darkness and rain made the evening's visibility poor, but he squinted through it and kept going. As he walked down the manicured hedgerows and over freshly mowed lawns the ground squelched beneath his feet, soaking his shoes and socks.

He reached the backyard and saw two men in a tight huddle. Tensions were high, and neither was happy about their need to have a chat. The first man was Charles.

Eric raised his weapon and stepped closer. "Steve Farrell. You're under arrest."

Farrell's head whipped around, and then he bolted.

Eric sprinted, bearing down on him at full speed. They broke through the trees and Eric heard someone on his tail, but he couldn't look back to see who it was. Farrell jumped a fence. Eric did the same, hitting the wet ground with a splash.

A car door slammed. Eric sprinted to the road and saw a Cadillac peel away. Someone landed behind Eric, and he turned to find Hailey had followed them.

"Where is he?" She was breathing heavy, just like he was.

Rain dripped from his ears. Eric leaned in so she could hear him. "He's gone."

He pulled out his phone and gave the details to Jonah, relaying that their escapee had headed east down the street, away from the center of town.

"This seems to be happening a lot today." Hailey's eyes betrayed her disappointment. "Let's go see Charles."

Eric grinned. "With pleasure."

Hailey trudged alongside him back to the house. The lawn wasn't so manicured now that his feet had left size-twelve prints all the way across it, but he didn't much care what Charles thought.

In fact, Eric had a few things he'd like to say to a man who'd abandoned his family in the process of trading in his wife for a newer model. Guys like that, who didn't realize what they had and threw it away, didn't deserve it in the first place.

Eric would've had a word with Charles, if it weren't for the fact Kerry would get scared, Hailey would get mad at him and the new wife would call the cops.

It didn't matter if Eric didn't know Hailey all that well, and hadn't met Kerry until today. No man worth anything did that to his family, even if he was the mayor.

They reached the front door. Hailey looked over and frowned. "What's wrong with you?"

Eric didn't really want to talk about it. "Long day?"

"Doesn't look like it's going to end anytime soon."

That was probably true, but Eric preferred it infinitely more than the quiet of his dingy apartment. His life had brought him here, and he could see why the team liked bringing in fugitives. Still, when he was all by himself, he wondered why God had done this to him.

Hailey studied his face under cover of the porch roof. "You look totally lost."

Eric looked at her. "Maybe I am."

He followed the hall to the kitchen. All the lights were on. Kerry was sitting on a stool at the breakfast bar. Wide-eyed and pale, she looked the way she had after Farrell's abduction attempt. Beth-Ann was wide-eyed, too, but she was staring at Parker, who stood in the corner with his feet hip-width apart and his arms folded, looking for all the world like a Roman centurion.

Parker lifted his chin. "You get him?"

Eric shook his head.

"Ames?"

"Just knocked out, it looks like," Eric said, "The ambulance came for him."

Parker nodded. "Good."

Eric turned to Kerry. "You okay?"

She nodded, still in shock. Eric could only guess how bad he looked, drenched and muddy as he was. He'd discarded the ball cap he'd been wearing earlier. At least his hair was short enough it looked the same dry or wet.

Hailey moved past him and hugged her daughter.

Eric turned back to Parker. "Where's Charles?"

The marshal motioned back down the hall. "Study."

Eric strode down the hall, though his shoes squished

on the wood floor with every step. He was probably leaving puddles. He sighed and opened the door to what he assumed was the study.

Charles was at the window, staring out at the dark with a glass of ice and amber-colored liquid in his hand. The ice clinked when he turned around. "You were at the marshal's office this afternoon, and on the street."

Eric nodded.

"I'll wait until Deputy Marshal Jonah Rivers gets here. I'll speak with him."

Eric folded his arms. "No, you won't. You'll speak with me."

Charles's salon-shaved jaw dropped. "Who do you think you—"

"I don't know you. I don't know this town and I'm too new to be tangled in the politics of who you are. That's why you're going to tell me how you know Steve Farrell and why he was here tonight after he attempted to abduct your daughter this afternoon."

"I am not some suspect for you to interrogate." Charles flung his arm out and his expensive drink sprayed onto the carpet. "I demand to speak with your superior."

Eric pressed his lips together to keep from smirking. It was like conversing with a spoiled child. "Why was Farrell here?"

"How would I know?"

"Maybe because I saw you talking with him in the yard."

Charles huffed. "The man is certifiable."

"It looked like a pretty heated conversation. What did he say to you?"

Hailey's voice came from the doorway. "Yes, Charles. What did he say to you?"

Charles's eyes narrowed on Hailey.

Eric said, "You can tell us here how you know Farrell and what he wanted. Or we can take you downtown and you can be questioned there as an accomplice to a fugitive. Either works for me."

Charles sputtered. Eric glanced at Hailey. Would she detain her ex-husband, or should Eric be the one to do it? At least that way, Charles wouldn't be able to claim Hailey had some kind of personal prejudice against him.

The phone on the desk rang.

Charles strode over and snapped it up. "Yes?" His eyes widened and his face paled. "How long do we have?"

EIGHT

Hailey stood with Eric while Charles argued with the person on the phone. A crowd of boots pounded down the hallway, and Jonah came into view with the rest of the team behind him.

He gave Hailey a short nod and his eyes narrowed on Charles. "Hang up the phone."

The mayor obeyed Jonah, dropping the phone like he'd just been given terminal news.

"Report."

Hailey didn't know who Jonah was talking to, so she took the lead. "Charles was talking with Farrell. We don't know why, or what about."

Jonah turned to her ex-husband. "Charles?"

It wasn't the first time Hailey was ashamed of him, and she was fairly certain it wouldn't be the last. Still, he was Kerry's father, so she stayed silent instead of chewing him out, which was what she wanted to do.

Charles scratched his jaw. It was what he did when he had to share bad news. "The dam is at capacity."

Eric glanced between them. "What does that mean?"

"They have to let out the excess, or the pressure will break the dam." Charles looked at his gold watch. "That means we're going to get an influx of water in about ten minutes—enough to flood the lower part of town." He snapped up the phone. "I have to alert the chief, and we need to get it out on the emergency broadcast system."

Hailey caught Eric's eyes and motioned to the door with her head. Jonah let them by and followed them outside, where the rest of the team had crowded around.

"Why are we letting him use the phone right now?" Eric threw his hands up and then let them drop back down. "He needs to tell us where Farrell is going."

Hailey shook her head. "He needs to concentrate on this right now. That man does not multitask. Trust me." She pushed out a breath. "Local emergency services are going to be diverted to help flood victims. If we're going to get Farrell in the middle of this, we have to do it ourselves. The BOLO is pretty much useless at this point."

Jonah nodded. "She's right. But Charles does need to tell us what he knows."

"Then maybe you need to ask your buddy what he knows, because Eric and I didn't get anywhere."

Jonah's eyebrows lifted and Eric glanced at Hailey.

"Sorry, sir. That was out of line."

"Yeah, it was. But he will tell me what we need to know." Jonah's gaze swept across the entire team. "Go home. Get your families either secured, or packed and out of town, and then get back here. You have two hours."

Everyone dispersed, but Hailey stayed with Eric and Jonah. She should check in with her dad, but she wanted to be there when Charles divulged what he knew. Not to mention she wasn't leaving Kerry. Not now. "How's Ames?"

Jonah adjusted his damp ball cap. "Paramedics said he has a pretty good bump on his head. They suspect a concussion."

Hailey nodded. "But Farrell didn't come here for Kerry, right? He came to talk to Charles."

"That's right."

They all turned to where Charles was standing at the door to his study.

Hailey studied his face. He looked older, and tired. "What does Farrell want?"

Charles swallowed. "He said this afternoon was a warning."

"Because Kerry got away?" Hailey was beyond proud of her daughter. She wanted to take out an ad in the newspaper to tell everyone that Kerry had kept a cool head, and she hadn't allowed herself to be put in the car. There was a fine line in dangerous situations like that. It could have gone wrong so easily, but it hadn't.

Thank You, God.

"But you didn't answer my question." Hailey pinned him with a stare. "What does Farrell want?"

"How should I know?"

"Oh, I don't know…" Hailey sneered. "Maybe because, of all the places he could have gone looking for whatever it is he wants, Farrell chose to come to you."

Charles looked like he was going to be sick. He'd never been a good liar, and she was counting on that now. Maybe he would tell her why Farrell had targeted Kerry. "Why do you think he's still here? He's after the jewels, and he won't stop until he has them."

First Deirdre and now Charles? "What do you know about the jewels?"

Charles blanched, but he didn't say anything.

Jonah shifted, turning his body more toward Charles. "Is he blackmailing you?"

Hailey was wondering that, too. Since Farrell's first move had been attempted abduction of the person closest to Charles.

Her ex-husband pressed his lips together.

Hailey rolled her eyes. "Come on, Charles. What is it? A payment, an old score, what?"

Charles's gaze flicked to her. The flash of guilt disappeared so fast she wondered if she'd even seen it. What was he hiding?

Face red, her ex-husband launched toward her. "You want to know why I didn't want you to become a cop? This is why!"

She put her hands on her hips. "Because I'm good at it, or because you had something to hide and you knew I'd eventually figure out what you'd done?"

There was no way she was going to let this go. Not when it put Kerry in danger.

Jonah lifted his hand to Charles's shoulder, but Charles backed up, his eyes on Hailey. "You think you're so good. So right and honest. But you're not! You want me to tell everyone all your secrets?"

"You're the one in the middle of this, not me. Don't you forget that." She didn't want the details of their marriage to be common knowledge, but there were more important things right now than responding to his threats. Hailey folded her arms. "Kerry is coming with me."

"It's *my* weekend."

"And despite the fact that I have a fugitive to catch, she will be safer at home with my dad than with you. I don't have time to babysit you, Charles. That's if you're not in a jail cell for the weekend."

"I can't go to jail! The town is flooding."

Hailey leaned toward him. "Maybe you should have thought about that before you decided to *lie to us*. You're hiding something, Charles. You think we won't figure out what ties you to Farrell?"

"Okay, okay." Jonah pushed her back. "This isn't getting us anywhere." He turned to Charles, which put his shoulder in front of Hailey's face. "Where did Farrell go?"

"How am I supposed to know?" Charles's voice was strained, like he was about to burst. "He just threatened me and then you guys ran him off. He didn't give me an itinerary."

Eric studied her, and Hailey saw a question in his eyes. A flicker of concern. She nodded, but he didn't seem to buy that she was fine. And why not? She held Eric's gaze, not backing down. She wasn't weak, and she didn't need to be coddled. It had been a long, rough day, and it wasn't over yet.

All this concern for her was going to get them both in trouble if it continued. Was he going to develop feelings for her? That would make their working partnership uncomfortable. Or maybe it was just concern shared between friends. It sure seemed like more, and it made her want to see what was underneath the "business" veneer he displayed at work.

But that would mean she was the one in trouble, the one with the feelings. The last thing Hailey needed after years of being single and being fine with it was to fall for a guy who was unobtainable, a guy who probably never even entertained the idea of there being something more between them. She'd end up the uncomfortable one, and he would never know. Because there was no way she would actually tell a guy she liked him—especially not a fellow marshal. That was a recipe for disaster.

She looked away, breaking the moment.

Charles huffed again, like the big baby he was. Hailey didn't need to wonder why she'd married him. After her dad kicked her out, Charles had been the only one who stuck by her. But surely there'd been a better option. Hadn't there? At the time she hadn't thought so.

"I don't know where Farrell went. All he said was he wants the money. Who knows what he's talking about? But he said if I don't give it to him by tomorrow morning he'll kill Beth-Ann and Kerry."

Senior deputy or not, Hailey pushed Jonah aside. "He said *what*?"

Charles actually looked guilty for the first time that night. "I'm sorry, Hailey."

She blinked. Had he ever once said that to her? She didn't think so. "Sorry or not, Kerry goes with me. Beth-Ann is your responsibility."

He nodded, and his shoulders slumped.

"If anything happens to them, this is on you."

"I'm not the only one at fault." Charles gritted his teeth. "Farrell is the fugitive, not me."

Hailey turned to Jonah. "Can I leave now? Because I'm not certain I won't shoot him if I stay."

Jonah's lips twitched. He looked at Eric. "Go with her and Kerry. You're on protection detail."

Eric frowned. "What about Farrell?"

"I'm nowhere near done asking Charles questions. The team will get Farrell. Your job is to protect Hailey and Kerry."

Eric drove, and Hailey sat in the backseat with Kerry.

"Did that escaped guy really come to see Dad?"

"It looks that way." Hailey's voice was soft. The way she spoke to her daughter was so different—it was like a whole new language they only spoke to each other. "Don't worry about it, okay? As long as you're safe, that's all that matters."

"But that guy is still out there. And what about the water? I heard Dad say the town was going to flood."

Eric's lips twitched. This kid was entirely too smart—

and nosy—for her own good. He hoped it didn't get her in trouble one day.

"Our house is on a hill. You'll be safe, and Eric and I are going to make sure Farrell doesn't get to you."

Eric took the turn for Hailey's house and started up the incline. He wasn't sure how he felt about standing on a ridge watching the town wash away. Not that he was worried about the small amount of stuff he'd dumped in his apartment, but not being in the thick of things didn't sit well with him. This was an all-hands-on-deck situation.

When Eric pulled onto the Westward Bridge, he slowed and peered out the window. In the dark he could see the water level was already high, and the runoff was pouring from the dam. It didn't look good.

The dam was old, and he wasn't confident it could hold out if the rain kept up. The last thing the town needed was for the dam to break and water to torrent down the valley. It would wash away the old town with the barest effort.

He would have to check the weather report for an update.

Eric took the turn and they hit the dirt road that ascended to the farmhouse where Hailey lived. The outside lights were on, and a ladder was against the siding. Eric had barely stopped before Hailey was out of the car, running across the front lawn.

NINE

Hailey hurdled over the flowerbed her mom had culti-vated, which was now full of weeds. "Dad!"

She heard the car door slam behind her.

"Dad, get down from there!" She squinted against the rain. It soaked her hair and ran down her neck. "What are you doing?"

Her dad labored down the ladder, step by step.

Kerry stopped beside her. "Grandpa, it's slippery."

Hailey waited until both his feet were on the ground and then folded her arms. "What are you doing?"

Alan Shelder was two inches shorter than Hailey. His face was lined with years of productive work that had now waned to slippers and a newspaper and tinkering in his work shed. "I'm nailing the windows shut, darlin'."

"You shouldn't be up a ladder, Dad. It's slick out."

"I did fine." He huffed and turned away, heading to his shed with Kerry following. He called back over his shoul-der, and Hailey saw something that might have been dis-comfort in his eyes. "Put the ladder away, will you, darlin'?"

"Sure, Dad." Hailey watched him walk. Was he feeling okay? He'd been a little under the weather lately.

She stepped up to the ladder, but Eric reached past her and grasped it instead. "I got it. Where do you want it?"

"In the garage."

Eric lifted it like it weighed nothing and retracted the top half. Hailey sighed, as the fatigue of the day pressed down on her shoulders. "I'll go make some coffee."

Eric trudged across the lawn with the ladder. "Sandwich wouldn't go amiss, either."

Hailey shook her head and went inside. She hung her jacket and kicked off her boots. Her jeans were soaked through, but she filled the carafe and measured out the grounds before she went upstairs to change.

It figured Eric would invite himself inside for a late supper. This marshal wasn't like anyone she'd ever met. Usually she tried to keep people at arm's length, especially men she didn't know all that well. But her dad probably wouldn't mind the company of another man. So long as Eric didn't get used to being there.

Sometimes it was like she and her dad didn't even speak the same language. If it wasn't for Kerry, Hailey didn't think they would see each other much, let alone share a house. It might be a sad fact, but Hailey figured they just loved each other in their own way. There was too much baggage now for them to get back what they'd had when Hailey was little—when her mom was alive.

In her room, Kerry was stretched out on her bed with her iPad. The twelve-year-old was probably messaging her friends.

When Hailey went back downstairs, Eric and her dad were shaking hands. She glanced between them. "Coffee?"

Her dad sat at the table, in the chair he'd occupied since his own father had died. "Sure, darlin'."

"Eric?"

"That would be great." He sat, too.

Hailey pulled out the fixings for a sandwich and set

them in front of him. She didn't mind feeding him, but if he wanted to eat he was going to have to make it himself.

She poured two coffees, set them in front of the men and then made tea for herself.

"So, Eric, you live around here?"

Eric looked up from his mound of turkey at Hailey's dad. "I have an apartment in town until I get settled. I love the land out here. It's so open."

"Been in our family six generations."

Eric's eyes widened.

He looked at Hailey and she shrugged. "That's only because we're all too stubborn to put up with carting our stuff anywhere else." She shook her head. "I don't even want to think about the generations of junk in the south barn."

Her dad took a sip of his coffee. "How about you, son? Any family?"

Eric's head dipped to the side in a sort of shrug. "Some. A twin brother in Texas with his wife, Mackenzie, and my foster mom lives in Florida with her sister."

Hailey swallowed. "Foster care?"

Eric nodded. "My mom left us with a neighbor and took off. My dad was in prison. He's out now, but he lives in California."

After a few minutes of silence, Hailey's dad sighed aloud and stood. "Well, kids. I'm going to hit the sack."

Hailey nearly laughed at his obvious attempt to give them "alone" time. She stood, too, and gave the grumpy old man a kiss on his cheek. "Good night, Dad."

"Nice to meet you, Eric."

"You too, sir."

Her dad trudged to the door. "It's Alan."

Hailey sat back down. Eric's plate was empty, and he was sipping his coffee. Hailey didn't know what to say, so she stared at the clock on the oven. And then the sink with the day's dishes in it.

"Your dad seems nice."

Hailey shrugged. "Sure. He's slowing down some, and chafing against it. I just remind him it's better than drooling in your pudding in some retirement home."

Eric laughed. "When you put it that way…"

Hailey returned his smile. "You get on with your brother?"

"He was always bigger, if not taller or older than me by more than two minutes. Aaron used to beat up the kids who picked on me. I feel a certain amount of appreciation for that." He smiled. "I went down for the wedding, but I haven't spoken to him much since I got here. We've both been busy, you know?"

The patter of Kerry's feet on the stairs preceded her barreling into the room.

"Tina says the whole town's been ordered to evacuate."

Hailey felt her eyes widen. "What?"

Kerry flipped on the radio they kept on the counter. "It's all over the airwaves, apparently. Doesn't matter where you are, they're ordering everyone to pack up and get out of town until the rain passes over. Head for high ground."

Hailey's dad trudged in. "We are on high ground."

Eric's lips twitched.

"We can't leave. We have to stay here." Hailey locked gazes with her dad. "The fugitive we're after has threatened Kerry."

Alan Shelder huffed. "I already called the chief and told him to send people up here. It's easier than leaving town. We should be safe from the flooding."

She gaped. "You turned our house into a safe zone?"

"Calm down, darlin'." Apparently he could tell she was ready to blow. "Your mom and I did the same thing, remember? And if it was good enough for her, then it's good enough for me."

She knew that, she'd even told Eric that, but these were totally different circumstances. Hailey turned to Kerry. "Go pack a bag."

Kerry rushed out of the kitchen while Hailey's dad put his hands on his hips. "Now what did you go and do that for? You don't think I want my family around me in an emergency?"

"What I want is for my house to be safe for *our* family. Not bring in a whole town's worth of people. Now we have to go, because if Farrell comes gunning for Kerry I don't want a bunch of people getting caught in the middle."

Eric cleared his throat. "I'm going to go in the living room and make some calls."

He stepped into the next room. He didn't really have any calls to make. But he pulled out his phone anyway, because it was better than witnessing the tension between Hailey and her dad.

He could hear Kerry moving around upstairs. Maybe Alan had a spare shirt he could borrow. It would be big on him, but it wouldn't be soaked through like the one he had on. A dry jacket would be nice, too.

Aaron had left a voice mail earlier, but Eric would have to wait a few days until life calmed down before he had time to chat with his brother. Then again, maybe a quick call was better.

He tapped the screen and waited for it to ring.

"What's up, brother? I thought you dropped off the map."

Eric smiled at the sound of Aaron's voice. "Nah, I've just been busy with work. We have an escapee, and there's a big storm. They think the town might flood."

"What?" Aaron sounded aghast. "Do you need help?"

"No." Certainly not Aaron's brand of help, which involved wading in and beating up whoever was picking on Eric. Until he'd been injured, Aaron had been a Delta Force soldier, which meant his protective instincts were a thousand times worse than a regular person's. What Eric needed was to help the team get Farrell and help the town through this flood.

"Are you sure? Because I can get up there if you need help."

"I can do my job, Aaron. I don't need you holding my hand." There was silence on the line. Eric squeezed his eyes shut. "Sorry. I shouldn't have said that."

"Was it the truth?"

It was Eric's turn to be quiet.

"Is that it, then? We just go our separate ways? I live my life and you live yours and we just send each other Christmas cards?"

Eric sighed. "That's not what I want."

"Then what do you want? You're not acting like yourself."

"Of course I'm not. I lost my job, and now I have this new life where nothing is right. Am I supposed to pretend I'm happy?"

"No, but—"

Eric squeezed the bridge of his nose. "Look, I shouldn't have called. I just didn't want you to think I was completely ignoring you. But I'm really busy right now and I need some time to…I don't know. Figure out my life, I guess."

"I'm sorry, Eric. I know you loved working in witness security."

"I don't need you to be sad for me, Aaron. It is what it is."

Aaron was quiet for a minute. Then he said, "What if God had this planned for you all along?"

That wasn't where Eric had wanted the conversation to go, especially not now that his brother was all gung-ho over his faith. "Aaron—"

"Hear me out, okay? You had a good life, but you still didn't have everything. Maybe God has more for you, but He had to move you out of the life you had so He could give it to you."

"I think if God wanted me to have more, He could have done it anywhere. He didn't have to bring me to this dumb little town in Oregon just to set me straight."

Eric ended the call and stuck his phone back in his pocket.

Something shifted behind him. He spun around, half expecting it to be Farrell. It had been that kind of day. Instead, Hailey and her dad watched him with identical looks on their faces.

Eric pressed his lips together. He wasn't going to apologize for how he felt about their town. Not when he'd lived in one big city or another all his life. He was going to try to settle here, but that didn't mean he had to like it.

Hailey turned away, disgust plain on her face. "I'm going to check on Kerry."

TEN

Eric watched her storm out and sighed. She could be mad at him all she wanted. They didn't have to agree about everything to work together.

Alan's eyes narrowed. "You best watch what you say about this town, son."

"Why? What's the big deal?"

Alan looked more than disappointed. "It might not always have been sunshine and roses, but my girl never left this town. Not once. It's home to her, but I guess you wouldn't understand that."

The old man strode away, leaving Eric with his morose thoughts. The truth was he didn't understand what tied someone to a certain place. Eric had lived all over, and he'd never felt at home anywhere in particular.

Home was the people you lived with. But now the only mom he'd ever known lived in Florida, his brother was building a new family of his own in Texas, and Eric was left with…what?

Was he supposed to be happy about being stuck here? Whether this was some grand plan of God's or not, the fact was he'd had something great and now it was gone.

Just like his relationship with Sarah. He'd been happy in Phoenix. Not over the moon, but as happy as you could be with a great job. There hadn't been much else since Sarah had been injured. The job had been everything to him, and now he didn't even have that.

Eric was determined to give fugitive apprehension his best effort, but that didn't mean he had to enjoy it. If Aaron was right and God had brought him here, then God was going to have to accept that Eric wasn't pleased about it. Because that was just the way it was.

Eric heard a screen slap back on its hinges at the back of the house. Whoever had gone outside was going to get wet. Probably not Kerry, since he didn't figure Alan or Hailey would have let her, so it was either Hailey or her dad out there. He should probably go check on them but figured neither wanted his company right now. And who could blame them?

He could barely stand himself half the time.

Hailey leaned against the back porch railing and stared out over the dark backyard. For the first time, her professional life had bled into her personal life.

Farrell had come after Kerry because of Charles, and now her dad had invited the whole town to stay at their house instead of evacuating. There was no way she could contain the situation with that many people hanging around. It would be too easy for Farrell to slip in and reach Kerry again.

Hailey's gut writhed and twisted like whipping flames, the heat seeping all the way to her palms and the top of her head. She curled her fingers on the peeling wood of the rail, knowing she couldn't lose it. That wasn't going to help anyone.

It meant a lot of compartmentalizing to not let on how she was feeling. Kerry didn't need to see her anger over Charles, or her stress about work. And it meant she was more focused on the job if she wasn't worried about home issues.

When she was home, Hailey wanted to be *home*. Until Kerry hit those teenage years when she wanted nothing to do with her parents, Hailey was going to soak up every bit of their relationship and give back to Kerry everything she could.

And that meant keeping her safe from Farrell, with Eric's help.

It shouldn't have stung to hear he didn't like the town, but it had. Hailey strove every day to keep it safe. People respected that, but they didn't understand it. She saw the looks she got at the grocery store or at church. They didn't know what drove her to want to catch criminals instead of volunteering for the PTA and teaching Sunday school.

The sound of car engines, a whole train of them, came from the front of the house. Hailey sighed. The two of them needed to ensure Kerry's safety and get somewhere they could all rest.

The door swung open behind her, and Eric stuck his head out. "The first of the evacuees are here."

Hailey nodded and followed him inside. Eric looked like he wanted to say something, but didn't know what. She hoped he wouldn't apologize, because she didn't like it when people did that just because you wanted them to and not because they actually meant it.

Her dad came out of the kitchen and then headed for the front door. Hailey saw the determination on his face and shook her head. "You should send them all away. What if Farrell comes here looking for us?"

"You know I'm not going to do that, darlin'."

Hailey trotted up the stairs to Kerry's room. It was pointless arguing with her dad. Eric could play host, but she didn't want anything to do with it. Not when they all saw something lacking in her.

Kerry's drawers hung open, and she was zipping up a duffel bag.

"Got everything?"

Kerry nodded. "I just need to find my red jacket."

"I think it's in the hall closet." Hailey reached for the bag and Kerry handed it over. "Are you doing okay? It's late. You must be tired."

Kerry shrugged, but there were dark shadows under her eyes. "I'm okay."

Hailey laid her hand where Kerry's neck met her shoulder and squeezed. "I know you are."

She grabbed Kerry's hand and led her downstairs. She'd never wanted this life for either of them, but she was so grateful to have Kerry that she wanted to drop to her knees and weep.

Conventional wisdom said Hailey should be looking for a husband to help raise her daughter—or so every old biddy in town insisted on telling her. But why did they have the monopoly on what was right? Hailey liked it that Kerry was her focus.

She did the best she could, but not much made up for the fact Kerry lived in two separate houses and alternated Christmases.

Perfect would have been so much better than just okay. This wasn't the way life and home was supposed to go. Hailey knew that much from looking at the other families at church with a mom and a dad and their kids all in a row. But the last thing she wanted was to have to divide her attention between her daughter and a romantic relationship.

Kerry took up every ounce of energy she had—that was just the way Hailey parented. And when she couldn't be there, her dad was an invaluable help. Unlike Hailey and her dad's relationship, Kerry loved spending time with her grandfather. It was as though, however he'd felt about her falling pregnant, that hadn't extended to Kerry as a person.

Hailey figured a husband would expect to be the center of her world, and she just couldn't see how that would ever work.

Eric was at the base of the stairs. "Car's already running."

"Good." As far as Hailey was concerned, the quicker they got out of there, the better.

He took Kerry's bag for her and Hailey grabbed Kerry's knee-length jacket. Kerry grabbed two umbrellas from the shelf in the hall closet and handed one to Hailey.

"Good thinking."

Kerry grinned. There was no way Hailey was going to let Farrell take that light away. She needed Kerry in her life to draw her out. Having a daughter had proved to Hailey that she wasn't the center of the universe. Not that she'd been overly self-centered before Kerry, but she had barely been out of her teenage years.

They stepped out into the downpour. Hailey could hear the sirens going off in town, the warning was loud and shrill enough to send anyone running.

Her dad's heart was in the right place, but she hoped the people crowding their front lawn with loaded-up trucks and RVs didn't take advantage of his hospitality. Or destroy the lawn too much with ruts from their tires.

Hailey nodded a couple of times to people she knew from around town. They seemed surprised she was leaving, but there was no time for her to explain. Hailey opened the rear door for Kerry and left her to put down her umbrella. She joined Eric at the back, where he had the trunk door up. She surveyed his collection of long, rectangular cases that held shotguns, rifles and a smaller case where he kept two handguns, and a stack of boxes of ammo.

She looked up. "I think we'll be good. You know, when war breaks out in the backwoods."

He didn't look too impressed with her attempt at humor. "You're the one who said we should be prepared."

"And you just happened to have all this in the back of your truck?"

"Can't leave it in my apartment, so I left it at work. I loaded up at the office earlier after Farrell tried to get Kerry. In case we get cut off."

This was about protecting her daughter? "Well, all right then."

Eric sighed, like Hailey was seriously testing his patience. "Can we get out of the rain now?"

The roar of rushing water swept the valley. Hailey spun around, but it was hard to see the town through the haze of rain. Who knew how long it would take the dam to overflow the banks of the river completely, and flood the lower part of town. Wherever they were going, it needed to be high ground they could get to fast.

"You want me to drive? I know a couple of good places we can go."

Eric shook his head. "Get in."

She chafed against his ordering her around, but walked around the car to the passenger side anyway. At the last second she got in the back instead, giving Kerry a smile like nothing was amiss. Kerry should have been with Charles that weekend. But if all this meant Hailey was getting extra time with her daughter, she was going to make the most of it.

Eric skirted his truck between a trailer with an ATV on it and a pickup before he pulled out down the road to town.

"So where are we headed?"

Eric kept two hands on the wheel, controlling the bounce of the soft ground. "Jonah called. He said to use his place tonight since he'll be out with the team."

Hailey blinked. "We're going to Jonah's house?"

"Yep."

She didn't even know where that was, but hopefully it was high up. The water level in town was only going to rise. Still, her brain spun with the idea of getting to see the personal side of her boss. She figured his house would be secure, since he'd been a marine before joining the marshals.

Hailey grinned. "He's giving us free rein of his house?"

"Uh…not exactly."

"What do you mean?"

"Well, he sort of kind of said don't touch anything. Or make a mess of any kind. We also have to feed his dog, and let him out."

She caught Eric's eyes in the rearview and saw his smirk. "Seriously?"

He laughed. "He was kind of adamant about the not-making-a-mess thing."

"Maybe we should take our chances with a motel."

"Or wear those booties they give you when you're working a crime scene."

Hailey laughed, longer and harder than usual because she was so tired. Kerry was smiling, so Hailey scooted to the middle and put her arm around her daughter. With her free hand, Hailey grabbed the middle seat belt and pulled it across her body to buckle up.

There was a huge crash, the sound like an explosion of metal hitting metal. Farrell's car slammed into the side of Eric's truck.

ELEVEN

Eric swam to the surface of consciousness and batted the airbag away. Farrell's car had destroyed almost the whole front end of his car. He touched his fingers to his top lip and saw blood there. That explained why his face hurt so much. His nose was probably broken.

He wrestled his door open. The intersection was deserted. The same Cadillac he'd seen at Charles's house was wedged against the front corner of his vehicle, the door open and the dome light on. The warning alarm was beeping. Farrell must have jumped out and left the keys in.

Eric fell onto asphalt covered with an inch of water, heaved himself up and pulled open the rear door where Kerry was sucking in deep breaths.

He handed her his cell phone. "Stay here. Do not move." He unlocked his phone and brought up his contacts. "Call Jonah and tell him what happened.

"I have to find your mom."

She nodded and he wished he could stay with her.

Eric scanned the area, nothing but a closed-down gas station and trees that bordered the road. He trotted around the car to Hailey's side where the door was open. But instead of her hanging out of the car, unconscious like Ames, there was no trace of her.

Where was she?

He pulled out the tail of his shirt and wiped the blood from his nose. With his weapon drawn, he checked once more that Kerry was fine and heard her on the phone telling Jonah what had happened. Eric headed for the trees closest to Hailey's side of the car, a straight shot from her door to cover. He pushed through and saw broken branches.

A man cried out, and then Hailey yelled.

Eric sped up, reaching the spot in the trees where Hailey and Farrell wrestled for her gun in the mud.

Eric planted his feet and raised his weapon. "Freeze!"

Hailey pulled on her weapon, but Farrell didn't release it. He lifted her up by her arms and slammed her onto the ground. "I'm going to kill you!"

"Farrell, let go of the gun."

"You shot him. I know one of you shot him." Eric saw a flash of pure rage on Farrell's face as he turned, still struggling to get to the gun. "I'm going to kill all of you!"

Eric held his weapon up as Hailey fought for possession of her gun. "Let go of it, Farrell. It's over."

The escapee's eyes moved to Eric, and his fingers released Hailey's gun. She backed up and trained her weapon on Farrell.

Eric kept his gun and his focus on Farrell. He asked Hailey, "You okay?"

"I was handling it."

"Yeah, it sure seemed like it." Eric shook his head, which hurt a lot. "You want the pleasure of cuffing this guy, or should I do it?"

"He tried to abduct Kerry. He's mine."

"It won't matter what you do with me. I'm still going to kill both of you." Farrell looked at Eric, then Hailey, and then back at Eric. "Which one of you shot him?"

She stepped forward and gave the order for Farrell to roll onto his stomach, holstered her weapon and palmed a set of cuffs. "What are you talking about?"

Farrell grunted as she pulled his arms back, struggling even though it was pointless. "At the airport," he said. "One of you shot him."

Farrell wanted to know which of them had fired at the airport. Either he or Hailey had killed someone. "Who did we kill?"

"He's not dead. Yet! And I want to know who did it."

He wasn't going to let Farrell fixate on Hailey. "It was—"

"Not our doing." Hailey hauled the guy to his feet, his hands now cuffed behind his back. "We were doing our jobs. Your friends were the ones breaking the law."

Farrell still had that enraged look on his face. "I'll kill your whole team anyway, just to be sure I get whoever shot him."

Hailey moved to lead Farrell back to the road, but Eric stopped him. "Who was shot?"

Hailey frowned. "Our priority here is taking Farrell in so he can be processed. Then he'll be off to California to serve out his sentences."

After Farrell was booked, Eric had every intention of taking a very long and very hot shower and sleeping for about twelve hours. After which he would eat an obscene amount of biscuits and gravy. But one look at Farrell's face said that wasn't going to happen anytime soon.

Eric waited until Farrell met his gaze. "Who?"

Farrell's eyes darkened further. "You're dead."

Hailey led him away, and Eric followed them with a sense of foreboding in his stomach.

Farrell was being detained, which would hamper his efforts to retaliate for the shots both Hailey and Eric had fired at the airport. Eric still wanted to know who Farrell was talking about, even if he understood Hailey wanting to check on Kerry.

The road was deserted and there was no sign of Jonah yet. A mud-splattered white sports car had pulled up.

Hailey froze. "Kerry?"

Deirdre Phelps stood with Kerry in front of her, a gun pointed at Kerry's head. What on earth was she doing out of police custody? Deirdre had been harboring a fugitive, after all. What was going on?

Eric pushed Hailey and Farrell aside. Hailey needed to keep her hold on their prisoner while he dealt with Deirdre.

Eric trained his weapon to the left of Kerry's ear, where Deirdre's shoulder was. "Put the gun down, Ms. Phelps."

"Let Steve go or I'll shoot her."

Eric didn't think she would shoot a child. Few people would ever pull the trigger on that one. Unless something or someone was forcing them to, which he suspected was what was going on with Deirdre. Was it Farrell?

Eric pinned her with his stare. "You won't get away with this. Let us help you figure it out."

"Let him go. That's it."

"We're not going to do that. You need to put the gun down before you make this worse than it is." Eric swallowed. "You don't want the death of a child on your conscience."

"I will kill her!"

Hailey made a noise in her throat, but Eric couldn't take the time to turn back and tell her she needed to keep her cool. She had to do that herself, and he knew she would.

"Put down the gun!"

Deirdre's hand shook. The last thing Eric wanted was for her gun to go off accidentally.

"Okay." He held up one hand. "Okay, Deirdre. I'm lowering my weapon. Lower yours, and we'll talk about this."

"Let him go."

A cold voice came from behind Eric, and Hailey said, "Let my daughter go, or I'll shoot him."

Hailey watched as Deirdre's eyes widened. Fatigue weighed heavy on her muscles, but the discomfort was nothing compared to the sight of someone pulling a gun on her daughter. Why wasn't Eric doing something? Hailey figured if she was going to get Kerry out of this, she'd have to do it herself.

"I said—"

"I heard you!" Deirdre's eyes flicked between Hailey and Farrell, as though she wasn't sure what to do. Apparently she'd run through her plan and was now improvising. Not good.

Deirdre shifted her feet and raised her chin. "Let Steve go, and I won't be forced to hurt your daughter."

Hailey tried to put on a brave face, even though she was shaking. Farrell had to feel it in her grip on his arm. She glanced at Eric's weapon, aimed right for Deirdre. "Put down your gun, Ms. Phelps. You're already in enough trouble without adding a murder charge to aiding an escaped fugitive."

This whole situation was like driving blindfolded. Except the person who kept getting hurt was Kerry.

Deirdre looked at Eric. "Put your gun down and I'll let her go. Give me my boyfriend and I'll walk out of here."

Farrell's body twitched like he was itching to run.

Eric nodded. "Done."

He lifted his free hand, palm out and took his finger from the trigger. Hailey knew it was still close enough he could get a shot off if he needed to. Eric was hardly going to disarm himself just because Deirdre asked. All they needed was for Deirdre to believe he had.

Deirdre looked at Hailey. "Let him go."

Hailey locked her jaw. "Let Kerry go."

After a second of silence and staring, Hailey shoved Farrell to the side and grabbed Kerry's hand, pulling her over. Kerry ran between Eric and Hailey to stand behind her mom.

Deirdre held her gun loosely, but she squared her gaze on Hailey. "Handcuff keys?"

"Don't push your luck."

Farrell's eyes were hard when he looked at her one last time. "The two of you are dead."

Deirdre revved the engine, and Farrell ran to climb in the passenger side. Dealer plates meant the car likely belonged on the lot of one of Deirdre's father's superstores. Which was probably exactly where she'd "borrowed" it from.

The sports car growled again and they sped away, leaving Farrell's car still steaming where it had smashed into Eric's SUV.

Eric strode forward and kicked the tire of his totaled vehicle.

Three federal cars tore around the corner, lights flashing. Hailey turned back to Kerry. Her daughter was drenched, her wet hair plastered to her head just like Hailey's.

Eric moved in front of them and Hailey looked up. His gaze was on Kerry. "You okay?"

Kerry nodded.

Jonah pulled up beside them in his car, while the other two cars continued on in pursuit of Deirdre and Farrell.

Jonah jumped out. "You ladies okay?"

Hailey gave him a look, but so long as Kerry was okay,

he could call her whatever he wanted. Hailey reached out and Kerry burrowed into her side. She squeezed her daughter tight and looked at Jonah.

There was something in his eyes she'd never seen before, a desperate grief that said he knew how fragile life was. He was happy for her, but that didn't mean something in him wasn't hurting. What was that about?

"Hanning?"

Eric didn't answer Jonah. His lips were still mashed together, befitting his mood.

"Let's head back to the law enforcement base of operations. You can tell me what happened on the way."

Eric led them to Jonah's car, and they climbed in, Hailey and Kerry in the back.

Eric was ready to close the door and get in front when Kerry reached out. She grabbed his sleeve and pulled him in so that he sandwiched her in between him and Hailey.

Kerry wrapped her fingers around Eric's sleeve, leaning her shoulder against his arm. He glanced up. The surprise on his face looked a whole lot like hope. Something was happening, something that put a lump in Hailey's throat.

She cleared her throat and leaned forward to speak to Jonah as he drove. "How is Deirdre out? Isn't she supposed to be in custody for aiding Farrell?"

Jonah shook his head. "Turner couldn't get the warrant. The judge evacuated like everyone else, and the jail is in the flood zone. She's supposed to be under house arrest until the streets clear."

Hailey sat back. "This is unbelievable."

"There wasn't time to tell you, what with Farrell being at Charles's house."

Hailey didn't even know what to say. Deirdre wasn't exactly the biggest threat, but the woman had just been holding a gun to her daughter's head.

Jonah said, "Tell me what happened back there."

Twice during the story Jonah pressed his lips together so hard they went white, but he didn't say anything. He also didn't criticize her for handling the situation instead of letting Eric do the negotiating. Hailey couldn't help but think that might be because he knew he'd have done the same thing.

"This is bigger than we thought if someone Farrell cares about is involved. We need to do more digging."

TWELVE

Kerry shifted and laid her head on Hailey's shoulder. Her breathing became deep and regular as Jonah took the least washed-out route through town. The low voice on the radio listed off roads now rendered impassable by the storm.

Eric turned from the window. "It won't help any of us if Deirdre and Farrell get caught in rushing water and have to be pulled out of their car. I hope the marshals in pursuit are okay."

Hailey nodded. "Me, too."

Jonah glanced back from the driver's seat. "Law enforcement has checkpoints at every major exit through town. If he tries to leave, they'll get him. I doubt he'll try to hike out. The mountains are impassable in this weather. He's more likely to get hit with a flash flood."

Jonah's phone rang. "Yes?" He listened to whoever it was while Hailey tried to ascertain if the news was good or bad. "Understood, sir."

He had to be talking to their boss, Marshal Turner. Hailey had no idea where the task force's most senior agent was, given they were in the middle of both a manhunt and a flood. She hoped for his sake the man was pitching in.

"Yes, sir." Jonah hung up and hit the lever for his blinker.

He turned off the road onto a hill that curved up to a warehouse. "Turner said the team caught up with Deirdre and Farrell. They ditched the car and cut across a field to the highway. The team pursued on foot, but someone in a van picked them up. No plates."

Hailey looked out the window. "Helicopter can't fly in this weather."

Jonah slammed his palm down on the steering wheel. "How is it they manage to escape at every turn?"

Hailey kept quiet. They needed to find out who was aiding Farrell. If something bigger was going on they needed to get to the bottom of it. Because bringing Farrell in wouldn't solve the problem, just one of the symptoms.

If Farrell really was after jewels, then they needed to look at cold cases. There had to be at least one in which the jewels that were stolen had never been recovered. Maybe it was still unsolved, even.

Why couldn't Charles have simply told Jonah the whole of what he knew?

Hailey loved looking into town history, especially old newspaper articles about the first marshals. Being part of an organization that had been around for more than a hundred years made her feel a deep connection with justice. Her great-great-grandfather had been a marshal himself, a decorated hero.

Hailey wanted that kind of recognition. If she found the person who'd helped Farrell escape, then people outside the team and her family would know she had done something important. Maybe, just maybe, this case might give her what she wanted.

Jonah pulled up in front of the warehouse where the law enforcement base had been set up.

Hailey realized she didn't even know if he was married. Jonah didn't wear a wedding ring, but that didn't always mean a man wasn't married. Charles never had, which wasn't surprising now. By the end of their marriage he'd stopped even bothering to hide his infidelity, almost like he'd been goading her into divorcing him. Not that Jonah seemed like the same kind of guy.

Hailey's door opened. She got out, and Jonah turned away to head into the warehouse. Eric got out of his side, lifting Kerry in his arms.

Hailey's heart hitched seeing a strong, good man holding her daughter. The scene arrested her so much that she could barely move. It hit her deep, where she had long ago buried the need to have a man help her care for Kerry.

Hailey had learned to cope without anyone but her dad to help. The cold, hard reality was that men didn't want strong, career-oriented women who carried guns and took down bad guys for a living. There was nothing nurturing or kind-hearted about that. Eventually she'd given up the dream of finding a man who understood her. Now she relied on herself, because no one could care for Kerry better than she could.

A bolt of lightning lit the sky, jerking her from her thoughts. Hailey raced to the door to get out of the rain. If anyone wanted to get to Kerry, they were going to have to go through her first.

Eric set Kerry down on a cot. How she could sleep when there was this much noise was a mystery, but she was resting at least. He, on the other hand, wanted to punch something. But he couldn't let the anger out, because that meant his emotions had won. The police station on the south end of town had flooded, so the local sheriff declared all the detainees should be moved to the county jail two towns over.

Police, sheriff's deputies and emergency response per-

sonnel all trudged in and out of the warehouse. It was
approaching two in the morning, but the coffeemaker
someone had set up in the corner was operating at maxi-
mum capacity, so the whole place smelled like roasted
beans. There were papers everywhere, half of them pictures of Farrell.

Deputy Marshal Turner held court in the corner, wearing his massive blue marshal's jacket. His chest was puffed
out with the knowledge he was the top federal dog in the
room. He spotted Eric and narrowed his eyes. "Hanning!"

Eric strode over. Hailey broke off from her conversation with Jonah and came to stand beside him, giving him
a conciliatory smile. He smiled back even though he didn't
feel it. This whole manhunt was playing out like a big joke,
and he didn't like being in the middle of it one bit. It was
like they'd been taken for a ride this whole time.

The only good thing was that it actually felt like maybe
he and Hailey were finding the partnership he'd offered
her in the beginning.

Eric faced his boss. "The flood is throwing a wrench in
the works of this whole operation. It's like Farrell's been
one step ahead of us since he escaped. Deputy Marshal
Shelder's daughter was almost abducted. All this talk about
a stash of jewels, or whatever it is, like it's just floating
around town—"

Eric gritted his teeth and tried to get some control. This
was his job now, and he was supposed to be able to just do
it and then go home. The job was not meant to have become a personal attack on Hailey's family.

Why couldn't he have been assigned to warrants instead of the task force? Picking up wanted criminals was
a whole lot simpler than this. At least then he could have
some kind of emotional distance from it.

"Deirdre Phelps was instrumental in Farrell's escape. Again."

Turner nodded. "We'll be on the lookout for her, too."

"And he mentioned a man who was shot the night of the escape." Eric paused for a beat. "I want to know what happened. Deirdre's supposed to be under house arrest, right?"

Eric's boss studied him, then clapped and rubbed his hands together. "Let's pay Thomas Phelps a visit. Find out why his daughter is helping an escaped fugitive when she should be packing up and evacuating like all the good citizens." He glanced at Hailey. "Bring me a cup of coffee to go, would you, darling?"

Turner strode away. Now the man suddenly wanted to be a real marshal again, instead of the desk-jockey he usually was?

"Hanning!" Turner waited at the door. "Get a move on!"

Eric strode over, ignoring the stares of every other law enforcement officer in the room. Hailey balanced a lidded paper cup on another and rested her chin on the top to hold them steady. Then she grabbed a third with her other hand. Eric waited until she'd caught up before taking the stack of two so that he was the one who gave Turner his cup.

They walked outside, and he held the front passenger door open for Hailey. "Marshal."

She grinned and climbed in, giving him a nod. "Marshal."

Turner shot Eric a baffled look and climbed in the backseat of the SUV.

Eric trudged around to the driver's door. "All righty, then. Evidently I'm the chauffeur." He climbed in the front.

Talking with Deirdre's father—who probably wasn't even in town anymore—was the last thing he wanted to do. Instead of Hailey, it was Jonah back at the warehouse with Kerry. All because Turner decided to go question a witness, and she didn't want to miss out on the action. Eric couldn't exactly have said no to either of them. Just for entirely different reasons.

They would have to keep a lookout. Farrell was determined to get revenge. Not that Jonah would allow Kerry to be put in harm's way. But Eric hadn't been able to help. Hailey had been the one who talked Deirdre down.

And why did that bother him? He'd been trying to keep her safe instead of making a wrong move and the worst happening.

Turner barked out directions that took them over water-logged roads to a car dealership. Thankfully it was halfway up an incline, since most of the town was under a foot of muddy water. The rain was still pounding down on every surface. Eric was so tired he didn't remember the last time he'd slept. Friday morning felt like days ago.

"The dealership?"

Turner smirked. "The captain always goes down with his ship."

Eric frowned, pulling right up to the overhang in front of the doors. He could see a light on inside. Turner jumped out first. Hailey opened her door at the same time as Eric, shooting him a grin.

"I'll take the back." Hailey peeled off to walk around the building.

Turner drew his weapon as they entered the building, so Eric did the same. He'd had his weapon out what felt like a hundred times today, while he hadn't pulled it out in a month of working WITSEC. Did Turner think Farrell was here? Maybe Deirdre's father had something to do with her helping Farrell escape custody yet again.

Eric and Turner worked their way through the show-room to the office. Eric didn't want any surprises. He was done with that for today. Or forever, actually. He yelled, "Thomas Phelps, this is the US Marshals!"

Turner flung open the door.

Thomas Phelps was in a chair behind his desk. The only light was dim and overhead. Eric could barely see anything. Thomas sat up when they entered, gasped and reached for something. When he lifted his hand, there was something dark in it.

"Gun!" Turner lifted his weapon.

Thomas James Phelps the Third dropped what was in his hand.

Marshal Turner fired his weapon three times. The noise deafened Eric, like a firework had been lit off right by his ear.

Phelps slumped in his chair as blood from the wounds soaked his shirt.

"Sir—" Eric didn't know what to say. He made his way around the desk and picked up what had fallen from Phelps's hand. "He had a cell phone."

Turner's eyes were hard. "It was a gun. It must have fallen under the desk."

Eric studied his boss. "Sir—"

"He had a gun, Hanning. That's all there is to this."

Turner didn't look guilty. He didn't seem to want to own up to what was a simple, tragic mistake. "Sir, I don't think—"

Marshal Turner lifted his weapon and pointed it at Eric. "He had a gun."

THIRTEEN

Eric stared down the barrel of Turner's gun, but his life didn't flash before his eyes. What struck him instead was that he was going to die here of all places. No one would know what had happened. Turner would walk and in the confusion of the flood all the evidence would be lost.

Turner would be able to write this up any way he wanted. While the reality was he'd likely brought Eric here for the sole purpose of pinning Phelps's death on him.

It really stunk being the new guy.

Don't come in, Hailey. Please tell me you did not hear the shot.

"Drop your gun on the floor."

Eric shifted, but he didn't set the gun down. Yet. "So you can shoot an unarmed man?"

He'd put his wet bulletproof vest on under the shirt he had borrowed from Alan, since the shirt was so big. Turner had to assume he was wearing one. Eric was surprised it hadn't soaked through, given how wet it was. But if he knew, that just meant Turner would shoot him in the head.

Not the way Eric wanted to go.

"I said, drop it!"

Eric turned the gun in his hand so it was horizontal, and lowered to a crouch. It galled him, but he set the gun on the floor, which was now covered with two inches of water.

"You won't get away with this."

It was a cliché, and Turner probably *would* get away with murdering Phelps and Eric, but Eric had to say something. After weeks of living in survival mode, he didn't want it to end like this. He wanted to know Hailey was safe and to make sure Kerry was okay. The thought jarred him, since he'd assumed his brother, Aaron, and Aaron's wife, Mackenzie, would be first on his mind. But it was his partner he didn't want to miss saying goodbye to, and there was no time to figure out why.

Turner's lips twitched. "There's no way I won't get away with this. You think I got where I am without planning, or taking steps to protect myself?"

That didn't sound good at all. "What have you done?"

"Only what anyone in my situation would do to make sure their retirement wasn't jeopardized." Turner sneered. "And now it's time for you to say goodbye, Hanning."

Eric shifted, ready to move. Running was futile, as was trying to sidestep a bullet travelling at eleven hundred feet per second. But he had to try. If he moved too early, Turner would adjust his aim and Eric would be a goner.

Hailey stepped in the room, her gun pointed at Turner. "I don't think so."

Turner swung his gun toward Hailey. Eric dived, slamming into her body just as the weapon discharged. Fire ripped through the outside of his left arm.

The roar of water, like a mighty wave breaking on a beach, swept the outside of the huge building. Above the sound of the rain pouring down, something crashed into the glass-fronted windows of the showroom. Eric hauled Hailey to her feet and they ran from Phelps's office across the forecourt.

Water surged through the showroom toward them, bringing with it a midsize cherry-red car.

Turner fired his gun again.

Eric looked back and saw their boss in the office doorway, his face angry. Eric pushed Hailey on and they sprinted for the exit with the car closing in on them. Eric pumped his arms and legs, not willing to admit defeat.

They tore across the slick tile floor and Hailey shoved open the glass doors.

Eric cut through the doorway half a second before the car sideswiped it.

Water bounced off the front windows, back across the lobby toward Turner. Eric pressed Hailey out into the angry night where the water was two feet deep. It was dank and full of the debris that had been washed through town.

His shins hit something solid and he stumbled over a wall of sandbags around the entrance. Visibility was horrible, but Eric pushed on using the few feet he could actually see as a guide. The SUV was on its side against the building, swept over like it weighed nothing.

He waded around to the rear. It took some heaving, but he got the back door open. The inside compartment, now above his head, was still closed. He flipped the latches on the storage space and caught the supplies when they fell out. The umbrella was useless, but he flipped on the Maglite. The beam cut through the dark night, though a flood light would have been better.

He pulled out his phone, but there was no signal. If Turner was still alive, Eric needed to get them both out of there.

He looked at Hailey. "We're going to have to walk across town."

* * *

Hailey waded beside him through the water. "What in the world just happened?"

Eric told her of Turner shooting Phelps and then turning the gun on him.

"He tried to kill you?" This was unbelievable. "I thought we were trying to find out how Deirdre managed to shake her house arrest."

"I know."

The weird thing was, Eric didn't look confused or angry. Not like she was. The corners of his lips were curled up. "What?"

He chuckled, wading beside her through the knee-high water. "We survived."

"We've been doing that a lot lately." A fact that didn't make her feel any better. "And I'm sort of sick of simply surviving. Not that I'd rather be dead. But when are we going to get the upper hand for once?"

Eric pulled out his phone. "Good question."

Water had roared from the west side of town, where the dam was, to the east end. Unable to see much because of the low clouds and heavy rain, Hailey's imagination filled in the gaps of the devastation that was surely impacting the whole town.

Eric tucked his phone away. "No signal. Maybe the dam had to be let out more. Or it could be that some equipment failed."

"So long as it holds. If it doesn't, the town will be washed away completely."

Eric was silent. Hailey looked over, confused at the dark look on his face. It seemed like so much more than the threat of destruction.

Eyes on the cloudy night sky, he said, "Why does everything end like that?"

"Badly?"

He nodded and then looked at her. "Happy endings aren't real."

Hailey sucked in a breath at the sadness on his face. "I don't believe that. I can't."

"Why not?" Something nasty flashed across Eric's face. She didn't think it was about her so much as it was his dislike of what he probably saw as naïveté and not hopeful strength. He looked away again. "There's no point in hoping. It doesn't do any good."

Hailey wanted to hug him, but she didn't think her co-worker would accept comfort right now. "I will never give up hoping, maybe not for me but definitely for Kerry. Anything is possible for her. And I want all the good and right and true in the world to be part of her future."

Eric stopped beside a brick building. "Just don't be disappointed when it doesn't happen."

Hailey let him have the last word on it. She leaned against the wall next to him as the heaviness of exhaustion weighed down her limbs, like the water which seemed to have soaked every part of her.

She checked her phone, trying not to get it any wetter than it was already. "The rain must be affecting the tower. It's probably intermittent, unless the whole tower is down. We should keep checking it."

There wasn't any reason to worry about Kerry, given she was both dry and in the place with the biggest law enforcement presence in the whole county.

He glanced up and down the street. "Where are we?"

"West end of town. When the phone signal comes back we should be able to call Jonah and get someone to come pick us up."

"You know what? I think we might be close to my place."

"Yeah?" Why was she oddly curious at the prospect of seeing where Eric lived?

"My apartment might be a good pit stop for a hot drink, some food and a bandage."

"A bandage?"

He shifted, and she saw the ragged tear in his sleeve, now matted with blood.

"You're shot? Why didn't you say something?" She tried to see it, but he swatted her hands away.

"Let's just get going. It isn't bad and there's nothing we can do with it when we have no supplies anyway."

Eric was soaked from the waist down. They probably could have moved faster through town if they'd swum. But he couldn't bring himself to suggest it, since that would mean immersing himself in the dank water.

Street lights were still on, and the water level was only to his knees. Every so often something floated past. Most of it, he didn't try to identify if it was trash or something worse.

Hailey glanced at him every few paces. To make sure he was still with her, or to make sure he was still upright?

Exhausted, Eric waded to a car and hauled himself up to sit on the hood. He leaned back against the windshield and closed his eyes against the pouring rain. If he lay there long enough, he'd probably fall asleep. Not a good plan.

He heard Hailey climb up beside him, but he didn't open his eyes.

He was pretty sure Turner had been hurt, if not killed, by the car crashing into the office door. But Eric wasn't going to push his luck by having them stay in one place too long. It wasn't worth the risk of Turner coming after them to finish what he'd started and catching Eric weaponless.

That was the main reason he wanted to stop by his apartment. He didn't feel right without a gun on his hip. Hailey was perfectly able to protect them both, but what kind of partner would he be if he made her take all the risk?

"The law enforcement command center is in the opposite direction, you know."

"Yes," Eric said. "But that's going upstream, which will take twice as long."

With a big sigh he hopped down, and they cut through a side street toward the road that ran behind his apartment complex. After that he only had to find his building in the maze of three-story apartments. When they got there, he could figure out why on earth his boss had just tried to kill him to cover up Phelps's murder. It was way too convenient.

Water rushed by them, making it harder to wade through. Eric could almost imagine he was fishing on a riverbank, except for the fact that he was freezing. Maybe when the weather cleared and they could take a day off, he'd ask Hailey if she and Kerry wanted to go fishing with him.

Eric's lips twitched, thinking of his hard-nosed partner in cut-off shorts and a T-shirt, holding a fishing pole. He chuckled.

"What?"

He looked at her. She was closer than he'd thought she would be, and for a moment the green of her eyes arrested him.

"Put me out of my misery, Hanning. What's so funny about this?" She motioned to the street at large with a sweep of her arm.

"You like fishing?"

"Sitting still, waiting for hours for a fickle creature to take your bait? No thanks."

"Yeah, I can see how fishing might not work for you."

He laughed. "I'm renting a top-floor apartment, so it's probably fine. As long as the whole building didn't soak up the river like cardboard and disintegrate."

FOURTEEN

Hailey stared out Eric's kitchen window. It was after six in the morning and rain was still falling at a pounding pace. The sun should have already risen above the horizon. Instead, the sky was almost completely black, the nascent day dawning dark and dreary. Dim light barely lit the apartment, which had no power. In fact, the whole block was out.

She decided to make a sandwich, but only for the sake of having something in her stomach. If she fell asleep at this point she wouldn't wake for hours, never mind what all broke loose. That was just the way her body worked. Sometimes it simply refused to listen to honest reason.

Eric's fridge held a pizza box, a case of soda, orange juice, coffee creamer and a half-empty gallon of milk. She found a jar at the very bottom of the door. The lid was crusted on, but she unscrewed it and found the dregs of what was supposed to be strawberry jam.

She spread it on the bread and forced it down. She wasn't going to risk drinking the orange juice. If Eric was anything like every man Hailey had ever met, he probably drank straight from the carton, and she wasn't going to go there. That was just nasty.

She grabbed a glass of water and looked at her phone for

the hundredth time. There was a signal. She found Jonah in her contacts and called him.

Eric's apartment was functional, but had absolutely no style whatsoever. It made her sad that his living space didn't have personality, but not sad enough to actually volunteer to help fix it. She doubted she'd be able to do better. Her dad's house was still decorated the way her mom had designed it.

She sat at his dinky little table and waited for Jonah to pick up.

"Rivers."

"It's Shelder. How's Kerry?"

"Still sleeping. What happened? You and Hanning disappeared with Turner hours ago."

Hailey related the story, giving him time to digest Eric's explanation of what happened. He'd have to tell Jonah himself and write a report, since she'd been coming in the back way, but this would do for now.

Jonah said, "Parker and Samuels are back at the office. We got word that Ames is awake. I sent Michaels to talk to him about how Farrell managed to get the drop on him outside Charles's house."

Eric trailed back from the bathroom. His button-down shirt was off, and he'd pulled on a clean T-shirt. With one hand holding gauze on his opposite shoulder, he came over and spilled what was in his arms onto the table. Bandages, more gauze and some kind of antiseptic cream.

"Uh… Shelder?"

She blinked and realized she was still on the phone with Jonah. "Yeah, um…yes. Sir. What?"

Eric's lips twitched. Jonah updated her on the manhunt and the search for Deirdre. Then he said, "Keep me apprised of the situation. When you're ready to move, I'll find you some transport."

"Got it."

"And when Kerry wakes up I'll have her call you."

"Great." Hailey hung up and tried not to look at Eric.

Personal feelings were generally frowned upon at work. And while two agents getting into a relationship technically wasn't against the rules, it also wasn't encouraged.

The marshals understood that it happened and they wanted to know when it did, but they didn't have to like it. Theirs wasn't a job where emotion helped. Not when they were chasing the most violent criminals.

They couldn't let their feelings for what the victims had been through cloud their attempts to bring the perpetrators to justice. Or their feelings for each other.

Hailey reiterated to her partner what Jonah had told her. She had to think of him like that. It would help to keep her feelings separated.

Eric said, "What about Farrell?"

"No sightings of him or Deirdre. Most everyone's caught up helping evacuate the town. Parker and Samuels are running computer searches to try and find a link between Farrell and Charles. And where this stash of jewelry might have come from."

"How about you?" Eric studied her. "Charles is involved, and you were married to the man. Do you know anything about that?"

Hailey grabbed the cream and squeezed it straight onto the clean gauze. Thankfully it wasn't more than a bad scratch. "I have no idea what they're looking for." She blew out a breath. "You know, I'm beginning to understand why Charles objected to being interrogated. I can't even believe you would ask me that."

Eric's lips curled up at the corners, but part of that might have been the pain of her mashing the gauze onto his arm.

"Deal with it, Shelder. You're part of this whether you like it or not. This case is personal, and you're involved."

Hailey didn't say anything. Eric held the gauze down and she began to wrap his arm.

"Maybe you should think about it some. In case you know something, but maybe you don't realize it."

"You think I've forgotten I know something about a stash of stolen jewels?"

"There's a chance, if Farrell and Charles really did know each other years ago. The timing might fit."

Hailey sighed. "Why does it feel like I've been put in the naughty corner?"

He laughed. "Let me guess, you were the teacher's pet?"

"I'll have you know I went to OSU on a full scholarship."

"Go Beavers?"

Hailey taped the gauze down.

"Married housing?"

She froze. "Excuse me?"

Eric really expected her to tell him she'd married Charles her junior year of college, had the baby early summer and then went back her senior year to graduate?

It had been hard every single step of the way, but she'd been determined that raising Kerry wouldn't set her education back. Having a baby wasn't a burden—it was a blessing. And being a mom to Kerry hadn't meant she had to give up her dreams, just that she'd needed to make some extra ones.

Hailey had worked twice as hard to graduate and make sure her child didn't miss out on too much in her first year of life. It had been Hailey's choice to stick with college, but she hadn't wanted Kerry to suffer for it.

Eric said, "I know we're not the kind of partners who share a lot of personal information, but I can't say I haven't been curious about you, and Charles and Kerry. We've been through a lot in a couple of days. I hope you know by now that you can trust me."

He had saved her life earlier, when Turner would have shot her. Still, Hailey felt her eyebrows rise. "Does that mean you're going to tell me something personal about you?"

Eric's smile dropped from his face.

"That's what I thought." Hailey turned away and heard Eric head back into his bedroom. Why did everything have to be so awkward between them?

She wandered around the tiny living room, tapping her fingers on the leg of her jeans while she tried to figure out what jewels Farrell was after. Anything to avoid the discomfort of conversing with her partner. Yes, a lot had happened in only a couple of days, but that didn't mean everything had to change.

Hailey seriously doubted Farrell would go to this much trouble to break out of marshal custody for something which might not be a sure thing. He must know where the jewels came from, or even where they'd been hidden—though he hadn't found them yet, apparently.

Deirdre had probably cut out from under her dad and her lawyer to pick up Farrell. Now they would never find him in this weather. As much as it irked her, Hailey was probably going to have to talk to Charles again. She needed the real story on why Farrell had gone over there to talk with him. There was no way that was a coincidence, not with the way Eric said they'd been arguing. She needed to find out the link between Charles and Farrell.

Since they'd known each other years ago, when Hailey had been in Charles's life full-time, perhaps she did have something. Maybe in the boxes of old stuff in her dad's attic. It was a long shot, but she didn't have any other ideas when the likelihood of Charles giving her a straight answer was slim to none. If Farrell was going to come after her daughter again, then both Hailey and Kerry were sitting ducks.

Her phone rang. Jonah's last name flashed on the screen. "Shelder."

"It's me." Kerry's voice was tired. "Did you really leave me on my own?"

Hailey looked at the closed bedroom door. When she put it like that, it sounded bad. "You're perfectly safe. I had to go with Eric."

Which, it turned out, was a good thing. They'd managed to save each other from getting shot by Turner.

"But you're not here to make me safe."

Hailey swelled with happiness, which was a little disturbing, considering the situation. She should be feeling thoroughly guilty at not being there for Kerry. But whenever the kid pretty much admitted she wanted to be with Hailey and no one else, she had to accept it no matter what was going on. She only wished the naysayers could hear her daughter now.

That was the downside of living in a small town. She'd become the local spectacle, a cautionary tale for young girls everywhere of what could happen when a person made poor decisions and let their life get out of control. Little did they know. She'd had her baby and still managed to finish college, all while holding her dream of a career intact.

She wouldn't trade Kerry's life for anything, but that didn't change the cold hard reality that she'd been young and careless about the consequences of her actions. Even though she'd worked it out herself…at least until the divorce, when it became plain she hadn't really worked anything out. She knew better now, hindsight and all that.

Kerry was growing into a fantastic young woman in her own right. But one who could wind up in the exact same situation, unless Hailey gave her the tools to be smart and keep safe. And to not wind up having to work twice as hard for what she wanted.

"You'll be okay." What Hailey meant was that Kerry would be safe.

"Why can't I go to Dad's?"

Hailey's lip curled. "It's not safe there. Everyone is evacuating." She couldn't let her feelings about her ex-husband take away from the fact Charles was Kerry's father. He might be selfish, but he wouldn't intentionally hurt his own daughter.

"What about Grandpa?"

"He's busy with the other evacuees."

Silence. Hailey didn't ever pretend to know what her daughter was thinking. She could barely remember what it was like to be that age, but figured she had probably been all about what teen boy band was hot at the time. Kerry didn't seem to be that interested in music, though. She listened to Christian radio, since Hailey's dad insisted they go to church.

Kerry huffed loud enough Hailey heard it even through the crackling phone line. Hailey could imagine her lips pressed into a fine line that was both hilarious and cute, even if it meant Kerry was upset. "What if I need saving? You'll be somewhere else, and you won't even know."

"Baby—"

"I want to come with you."

"You can't, Kerry. Farrell tried to kidnap you yesterday and he said he's going to kill me and Eric. I want you surrounded by people who can protect you."

"They have badges and guns, but they aren't you. They don't care about me like you do."

Hailey stilled. "That's true."

"Then come back and get me."

"I'll talk to Jonah. Maybe we can work something out."

Kerry jumped in immediately with her response. "You can stay with me?"

"Maybe. We'll have to figure it out."

Kerry hesitated. "Is Eric your boyfriend?"

Hailey glanced over her shoulder, but Eric hadn't reappeared. She lowered her voice anyway. "No, Eric is not my boyfriend. He's my partner."

"Don't you like him?"

Hailey shook her head. "Where is this coming from?"

"I don't know. I just think…you've never had a boyfriend. That I know of. Maybe you want to think about it. Eric seems nice." Kerry gasped. "Maybe he likes you!"

Hailey shook her head at her daughter's exuberance. "That's sweet, but I don't think he does. We just work together."

Kerry paused. Did she not believe her? "Seriously, Kerry. I don't think he feels that way about me."

"So you do like him?"

Hailey sighed. "Are you trying to set me up? I'm not worried about being an old maid. That's not even a thing anymore. I don't need to have a boyfriend."

"But Dad is married. You might like it if you tried it."

Hailey almost laughed. "Your dad is happy in his own way, but that doesn't mean I have to get married, too. I can be happy with just you."

Since the divorce that was exactly the reasoning she'd used to convince herself she didn't need a man in her life. She could be whole without one. But did Kerry spend time with Charles and Beth-Ann, and then come home to Hailey's house and see what was missing in her mom's life?

"Do you think we need another guy around? Isn't your grandpa enough?"

Kerry didn't understand the risks of dating. Guys would say anything, and the reality often turned out to be something quite different. She'd seen it with friends over and over again. But fear was only part of what held Hailey back.

Charles hadn't cared about her at all really, even though he'd supported her financially. Most of that was probably because he'd known he was headed for politics, and even back then he was determined to protect his reputation. His father likely convinced him of that, given how many times Hailey had heard the old man's lecture about keeping his nose clean.

Kerry said, "Maybe while you're with Eric, you should think about it. Like flirt a bit, and see what he does."

"Flirt?" Hailey choked.

"If he likes you, he'll flirt back. Then he might ask you out to dinner." Kerry's voice danced with delight. "Maybe he's *the one*. That would be so romantic!"

Hailey rolled her eyes, thankful her daughter couldn't see her face. "Okay, okay. Let's not get ahead of ourselves."

"So you'll do it?"

"I'll think about it."

Kerry groaned. "That always means no."

FIFTEEN

In the bedroom of his apartment, Eric could almost pretend there wasn't a natural disaster going on outside, especially when his arm burned like a hot poker. Not that he knew what a hot poker felt like, but he could imagine.

He put on a clean shirt and jacket, took a couple of over-the-counter pain pills and then came out to where Hailey was staring out the kitchen window again.

Eric needed to make sure she got through this in one piece. He wanted his partner to be okay for her daughter's sake—and for her dad's, even though their relationship seemed tense.

Under her tough exterior he was starting to think there was a woman who'd been burned one too many times. Maybe it was because of the damage Charles had done to her emotions.

There weren't many other things that might have caused Hailey to be so closed off with anyone and everyone except her daughter. Eric had loved once, and deeply. He'd been engaged to Sarah when she was shot, and her subsequent rejection of him had left its own wound.

Eric's phone lit up, vibrating across the kitchen counter. The signal he'd lost must have come back. "Hello?"

"Eric? Can you hear me? Are you there?"

He groaned at the sound of his brother's voice. "You need something? I'm kind of busy." If the definition of busy was standing in his kitchen, essentially doing nothing. There was silence on the line. "Look, I shouldn't snap at you. Sorry."

"Did you get hurt?"

Eric glanced at the bandage on his arm. "How'd you know?"

"You think I don't know you only get mad when you're in pain?" Aaron sighed. "What happened?"

My boss tried to kill me. Eric didn't need his brother riding in on some motorized steed to save the day. It might have been helpful when a pack of older boys were beating the snot out of Eric in his braces and glasses. But he was a grown man now, one who didn't need his twin acting like a big brother who had to take care of him.

Since the day Aaron left for the army, Eric had figured out how to take care of himself on his own, and he'd done fine all these years.

Eric's jaw was so tense it cramped. "We're taking care of it."

Aaron muttered over the phone line, but all Eric caught was "Stubborn."

Yeah, she was. Hailey was leaning against the wall with her arms folded, not bothering to pretend she wasn't listening to his end of the phone call.

Still, Eric didn't think that was what his brother meant. "My partner and I are going to be back at it soon. I should go."

"You're really not going to tell me?" Aaron paused. "I can pray for you better if I know what's going on."

Eric sighed. If Aaron wanted to pull out the big guns then he'd give him what he wanted. "My boss killed a man and then tried to kill me. I'm pretty sure he was going to frame me for murder. You know, posthumously. The whole town is flooded, and I've got a bullet graze on my arm that hurts like crazy."

Hailey's eyebrows rose.

Aaron yelled, "You were shot?"

"You'll remember that I didn't want to tell you. I'm okay, Aaron. I don't need you to come up and babysit me. It would take you hours to get here, anyway. It'll probably all be over before then."

"And…if I was already on my way?"

Eric's stomach churned. "You aren't. You wouldn't— where are you?"

"I caught a flight, but I'm stuck in Portland. No one's going any closer to you, with the weather being like it is. I'm going to rent a car and drive as far as I can."

Eric groaned, ignoring the fact Hailey was chuckling. "You might want to nab a Jet Ski while you're there. That's the only way you're going to get around town with any ease."

"Noted."

Eric sighed. "You don't need to come."

"This is an intense situation. It isn't just about your job. It's about the whole town. And if you think I'm going to stand by and let something happen to my son's Uncle Eric, you're crazy. That kid's going to need all the family he can get."

"Mackenzie's pregnant?"

Aaron laughed. "That's pretty much the reaction I had. Can you imagine me as a father? Cleaning up baby puke, and changing diapers?"

Eric laughed, too. "Now, that I would pay money to see."

"There's the brother I know."

Eric sobered pretty quickly, but he didn't say anything.

"I know getting moved out of WITSEC was awful, but I thought you'd take some time and find the good in this transfer. Instead you've been moping for weeks."

Eric rolled his eyes. "Thanks, brother."

"You know what I mean. You used to be fun. Confident. It's like you slipped back into…"

"I know." Eric gripped the edge of the counter, turning away from Hailey's gaze.

The days after he'd finally accepted the fact he had to let Sarah go were dark, to say the least. He'd forgotten how dark—probably because he'd been trying not to remember it at all.

He didn't look at Hailey. "I'm sorry. I really tried not to mope, but it feels like I'm drowning. I can fight all you want me to, but it makes it worse."

"I'm glad you're back."

"I'm not. Not completely," he said quietly. "But I think I might be getting there."

And he was. Protecting Hailey and Kerry gave Eric a sense of purpose he hadn't felt since the plane had touched down in Oregon. But his brother didn't need to know it was because of a woman that Eric was better. Aaron would get the wrong idea about that.

Eric might find Hailey attractive in a completely exasperating way, but that didn't mean he wanted a relationship. He was not good at those at all. Eric didn't know what Sarah had seen in him. Evidently it'd been enough for them to build a future, but not enough to survive her being paralyzed.

"So I'll call and let you know when I'm close to town. Okay?"

"Yeah." Eric sighed. "See ya."

"Bye."

He set the phone down. He didn't want to be at odds

with Aaron. His brother demanded too much, and it was a price Eric was honestly scared to pay. Being that vulnerable wasn't something he wanted to go back to, not when Eric was trying his hardest to stand up for himself. He might be a US marshal, but Aaron made him feel like the chubby, nerdy twin who needed protecting.

Stomach tight, Eric turned, ready for the barrage of personal questions that was sure to come.

Instead, Hailey pushed a wet hank of hair from her forehead and put her hand on her hip. "What's up?"

Eric laughed, relieved she wasn't going to push this. "I'm an awful host. I've been so worried about the bandage and feeding myself, I didn't even think about the fact you're soaking wet. I'll get you a towel."

He went to the closet and pulled out one of the purple ones his foster mom had sent, the ones he'd never used, and handed it to her. "Did you get something to eat?"

Hailey squeezed out her hair. "I had a jam sandwich."

"How's Kerry?"

She wrinkled her nose. "Not happy, but she's safe and has plenty of people to watch her. When she saw some of her friends, kids of cops and firefighters, she was happy. She told—"

The phone on the counter, Hailey's cell, rang but cut off before she could grab it.

"No service." She shook her head, and then said, "Kerry told me she'd see me later, when you and I get back."

A smile played about her lips. There was something there that she didn't want to tell him. But for some reason, he was fine not knowing. He liked the close relationship she had with her daughter.

The gleam of a secret in her eyes drew him in, so that before he knew it he was standing in front of her.

Eric leaned down and touched his lips to hers in a quick, light kiss. "Thank you for being here with me."

Hailey stared at her partner, the warmth of his touch still lingering on her mouth. Apparently flirting had gotten a lot easier in the decade-plus since she'd last done it, because all she'd done was stand there and he'd given her a sweet kiss. She'd never in her life been the recipient of a kiss like that. A simple gesture, meant only as thank-you.

Hailey's eyes burned, she'd been staring at him for so long. She blinked. "What was that?"

"Thank you. Like I said."

"You couldn't just say it?"

"Sometimes showing is better." His smile dropped. "I'm sorry. I guess I shouldn't have done that."

He turned and went to the kitchen, but not before she saw a frown mar his handsome features. Perturbed was not a good look for him.

Hailey stared at his back, feeling like whatever had just happened could have ended a whole lot better than that. Why did she have to question it? She was only surprised, and he'd thought that meant she wasn't okay with it. Who apologized for kissing someone? It hadn't felt forward. It had been…good. Maybe not swoonworthy, but there had been a definite spark that could be worth exploring.

"Hot chocolate?"

She blinked. "Uh…what?"

Eric turned to her. He was wearing his socks, which was unnerving to say the least. "I figured you've probably had your fill of coffee by now. How about hot chocolate?" He lifted a white packet and shook it. "It's the kind with the marshmallows already in."

She strode to the breakfast bar that separated the tiny kitchen from the living room. It had just been a friendly kiss. She shouldn't make a big deal about it, especially when she was only hyperalert because of her conversation with Kerry. The idea of her flirting was laughable. She was so rusty at relationships it was almost ridiculous.

She squelched onto a bar stool and winced. "I'm a little soaked."

"I'd let you borrow some clothes, but they'll be six sizes too big." He shook his head like this really bothered him. "I'm sorry. Here I am all dry and you're still soaked."

She returned his smile. "I've been in worse situations than this. And it's better than running after a fugitive in a T-shirt hanging past my knees."

Eric turned back with two hot cups—apparently it was "to-go" hot chocolate—and caught her staring. His eyes went wide and Hailey bit her lip to keep herself from wincing. She hopped off the stool, praying this wouldn't get weird. It was best if they halted it here. Otherwise she'd end up transferring back to court duty. She would grow old and gray, eating donuts at the security station just inside the courthouse door.

It was enough to make her shudder.

She grabbed her phone again. "There's a solid signal now. I'll call Jonah and see what the plan is."

Two minutes later they had instructions to wait for the sheriff's department to take them to Jonah's house, where he had a fishing boat they could use.

"Let me get you a better jacket." He disappeared into the bedroom again, and returned with a man's raincoat. "It'll hang to your knees too, but at least you'll be covered."

"Thank you." Hailey slipped it on, marveling that there was a male deputy marshal actually capable of being considerate without making it sound like she was helpless just because she was a woman.

Eric pulled a lockbox from under the couch and loaded

his pistol, which he tucked into a shoulder holster. He returned the lockbox to its place and closed up the apartment while she waited under the cover provided by the edge of the roof. The sheriff's department was here.

Within an hour, they had Jonah's boat and a spare radio he'd had in his garage. Hailey plugged in the radio and it crackled. The noise outside was so loud she plugged in the earpiece Jonah had given her with it.

"Base, this is three-sixty-five. Say again. Over." It grated her to use the code, but safety was important, and keeping their identities to themselves—even on the off-chance someone might be listening—could keep Farrell from knowing their locations.

Jonah's voice came through, right in her ear. "Situation report, three-sixty-five."

Hailey thumbed the volume down. "Base, we're headed back to you now. Over."

"Negative, three-sixty-five." Hailey frowned at Eric as she listened. "Return to the office for an update."

"Copy that, base."

Hailey looked at Eric again. He was sitting in the back, piloting the boat. "Jonah said to go back to the office, not the warehouse."

"For what?"

"An update, whatever that means." She sighed. "Kerry has my backpack. I was going to change my clothes."

Eric shot her a commiserating smile.

"Twice as far in the wrong direction? This better be good."

Eric nodded and took a sip from his hot cup.

The water level was much higher now, even though they'd been in Eric's apartment barely an hour. When they reached the office the entire bottom floor was underwater, so they parked the boat by the fire exit and tied it up. Two flights of stairs later, they tried the door. It was locked.

Eric looked at her. "You have your swipe card?"

Hailey shook her head.

"Me neither. Aren't Parker and Samuels supposed to be here?" Eric hammered on the door.

Parker and Samuels came into view, their weapons aimed at Eric and Hailey.

SIXTEEN

Hailey had figured the door was made of bulletproof glass, but maybe it wasn't. She and Eric both raised their hands. Parker unlocked the door to the office, and neither of the men holstered their weapons until they were inside. "We've had some looters in here trying to get at our weapon stash."

"You held them off?" Hailey looked impressed.

Parker grinned. "No, I just told them if they didn't leave I'd dump them in witness protection in the Louisiana bayou where no one would be able to hear them scream. Stupid kids are more scared of gators than they are of me." Parker led the way to his desk. "Come see what we found."

Hailey glanced at Eric, who seemed bewildered by their teammate mentioning gators in one breath and then moving back to business in the next.

Maybe Eric didn't know Parker had been a Navy SEAL before he joined the marshals. The man was an adrenaline junkie who got tired of routine easily and needed a new challenge about every five seconds.

Parker stood behind his chair, like he had entirely too much energy to sit at a time like this. "It took some digging, but we found out that Farrell's brother was recently released from jail."

Hailey nudged the chair back and sat. On screen was a file for Roger Harmer—same long hair as Farrell and a similar rap sheet. "He's halfway through a ten-year sentence in Washington for armed robbery."

"Actually, he was eligible for parole a month ago. I called the prison and was told Roger Harmer got out on probation."

Eric shifted behind Hailey's shoulder. "And they're brothers, you said?"

Parker nodded. "Harmer is older. He was placed in foster care as a baby and eventually adopted. Farrell was born six years later. Farrell lived with his mom until she died of an overdose before he finished high school—"

"Which he never did," Hailey said. "So is the brother here? Harmer was probably on the team that helped Farrell escape. The man that Farrell mentioned had been shot, maybe?"

"I can't believe he was let out and we didn't even get word." Parker shook his head. "He was picked up outside the prison. We have surveillance photos coming over to see if it was maybe Deirdre, or someone else connected with them, who picked him up. No one's seen him since, and he never checked in with his parole officer. If things were normal around here we'd be coming in on Monday to this guy's file."

"So they could be working together. Or this could be a completely irrelevant—although fascinating—tale." Hailey turned the chair around and folded her arms. "How do we know they're linked, other than a biological relationship? The last thing we need right now is a wild-goose chase. We have to be right."

Parker's eyebrows rose, like she should know better than to question his work. "Roger Harmer has a condo in the same gated community as Deirdre's townhouse. It was rented out while he was in prison, but his name is on the mailbox. Oh, and in case you were wondering, Thomas Phelps owns Roger's condo."

Hailey shot a glance at Eric. "And now Thomas Phelps is dead."

Jonah had advised Hailey and Eric to keep under wraps the fact Turner had killed Phelps and then tried to kill them. But they'd had to tell the team Phelps was dead. Not even a BOLO had gone out for Turner, since Jonah wanted to keep what had happened locked down. Their team leader had simply put word out that they'd discovered the body and then parted ways.

Jonah's instructions were that whoever caught up with Turner should bring him back to the command center at the warehouse, but not to say why they wanted him there.

After the flood waters receded they could figure out what had happened, since right now their priority was the team's safety and the search for Farrell.

It wasn't that they didn't believe Eric's story about Turner pulling the gun. The issue was the fact no one had discovered Phelps's body, the lack of evidence, the two opposing accounts—and the question of why Turner had done it. They didn't want to spook him if there was more going on, but they also didn't want him to disappear.

Eric nodded to her. "We should hit that condo. See if we can find anything."

Hailey stood. "Let's go."

"Want some company?" Hailey saw Parker's face and knew he was itching to get out of the office.

"Sorry. Jonah assigned you guys here." She added a pout to her smile just to irk him.

Parker's lip curled. "You get to have all the fun."

She laughed. "And you get to stay dry."

"That doesn't mean I'm not hungry." Hailey and Eric

strode to the door and Parker yelled, "Next time bring a steak."

Right before the door shut, Hailey yelled back, "Maybe I would have if you hadn't eaten Eric's pizza."

Eric chuckled. They took the stairs two at a time on the way down.

Hailey untied the boat. "Oh, look. It's still raining."

Eric chuckled. "It's just a sprinkle. It'll pass."

Hailey hoped it would pass soon, because the water level was higher than before. The rain was still falling as hard as it had been all week. She doubted she'd be able to walk in it if they capsized, and where would they be then? As thinly spread as the team already was, they would never catch Farrell and bring Deirdre in, or round up their newest client—Farrell's brother.

Eric couldn't believe this was the same community they'd been in only the day before, looking for Farrell at Deirdre's house.

"Looks different, huh."

Eric met her gaze and smiled, powering the boat through the streets. "I was thinking the same thing."

The streets were a river of water, and as they motored through the open gate, Hailey scanned the houses using his flashlight. The power was out, but he didn't see signs of anyone in the residences or on the street. The rain had eased off, but not by much. They were both still soaked, though Hailey more so since she hadn't changed.

He powered the boat through the streets of Deirdre's neighborhood to the address. Hailey looked down at the paper Parker had given her. "Take a right here. Should be two buildings down on the left."

Eric turned the corner.

"Front door's wide open."

"I see it," Eric said.

He cut the power by the front steps, and Hailey jumped out to secure the boat to a railing. Weapons drawn, they entered the residence together as though they'd done it a thousand times.

This night had brought them closer than he'd expected. They'd come up against the target, and in the midst of the destruction of the town, Eric couldn't help but realize something. He'd offered Hailey a partnership, and while she'd hesitated—turning him down, for all intents and purposes—the trust they had built since then had been worth it. Hailey wanted him around as much as he was starting to want her with him.

The house was a mess. Roger Harmer's basement garage was completely flooded. If it was anything like the first floor, there would likely be more junk than water down there. The soggy hall carpet was covered with trash, newspapers and empty pizza boxes, but it was the smell that got Eric every single time.

There was nothing else in the world that smelled like death. Hailey glanced back at him. Her eyes were shadowed from the lack of light, but he could see her discomfort. She smelled it, too.

"Let's find the body."

Hailey nodded, and they continued to search the house. Roger Harmer was in the bedroom, apparently having expired sometime between Farrell hitting them with his car and now. Harmer must have been the person they both fired on at the airport, but he hadn't been dead when Deirdre held her gun on Kerry and escaped with Farrell. It must have happened within the last day. And from the look of it, Roger Harmer had not died peacefully of the wounds he sustained from the shot that had hit him.

Maybe it was a blessing they wouldn't know who was ultimately responsible for his death.

When they had cleared every room, Hailey turned to Eric.

Before she could say it, he said, "I'll call it in."

Hailey nodded. They now had a concrete link between their escapee and his half-brother.

Eric informed Jonah, who said he would pass the news on to the local law enforcement officers to process the scene. Then he trailed behind Hailey down the stairs. "Police are on their way. You want to wait outside?"

Hailey shrugged and followed Eric back down.

He headed into the living room instead. "Are you okay?"

She didn't say anything. She just slumped onto the couch and shut her eyes, looking more tired than he'd ever seen. Eric couldn't relax. All he could see was Phelps in that chair behind the desk, and then Turner pointing his weapon at him. At Hailey.

"First Thomas Phelps, and now Harmer?" Eric looked up at Hailey. "You think Turner could be involved in this, too? Maybe he was on the assault team."

Hailey's eyes widened. "I don't want to believe it of another marshal, but I guess it's possible. There's no way we're going to find out in this flood, but he could've been part of the team that helped Farrell escape. Too bad he could be anywhere. Long gone, even."

Eric ran a hand through his short hair and felt the water run down the back of his neck. "So now we have two guys and Deirdre to find out there, and we're stretched thin in the middle of a natural disaster. Things keep getting worse and worse."

Hailey looked like she wanted to laugh.

Eric frowned. "There's nothing funny about any of this."

"It's going to take a whole lot of cleaning up."

Eric squeezed the bridge of his nose. "The police will take care of Harmer. He's under their purview, since we don't investigate murders. We're still on Farrell. And we don't even know if Turner is involved, though it's not looking good for him. Deirdre and Turner will turn up. Jonah will take care of that. What do you think?"

She needed to know that he trusted her instincts.

Hailey's face flushed. Apparently she'd been expecting him to take over and dictate their moves, but he wanted them to figure this out together. "My guess would be that the lack of medical attention killed him. The location of the wound means he would have been in pain for hours before he died."

Eric crouched in front of her. "We don't know who shot him."

Hailey didn't say anything.

"He was helping a federal fugitive escape and you and I were just doing our jobs. That's all there is to it."

She nodded.

"We should concentrate on Farrell. At least until the town is put back to rights."

Hailey's phone rang. She glanced at the screen and blew out a breath. "It's my dad."

"I'll go outside and direct the cops." Eric stood at the door with his flashlight, but he didn't close it.

Hailey's voice was full of emotion. "Yeah, Dad." She paused. "There are people everywhere, right? What does it matter if some kids want to fool around in the backyard… I know that, Dad, but I can't check it out right now. Isn't there anyone there who can…? Okay. Fine."

Eric winced as she huffed out another breath.

"I'll see what I can do." Hailey strode over to join Eric at the door.

"Problems?"

She rolled her eyes. "Some kids messing around at the house. He wants me to check it out, like I can just drop everything in the middle of the storm of the decade and go have a chat with bored teenagers."

Something niggled at Eric. "Does he call you like that a lot?"

A frown flickered over Hailey's brow. "No. Not really."

"You don't think he knows you're busy?" Eric held her gaze. "Would he call if it were just kids messing around?"

Hailey looked away, her eyes dark with something he didn't understand. He'd never really had to worry about parent/child dynamics, so he didn't know how it worked when you were an adult trying to maintain a relationship like that.

Eric said, "My mom left my brother and me with the neighbor for two days until they finally called the cops. She was across town getting high, and we had nothing to eat and no way to get into our house for clean clothes or anything."

He didn't want to get mad, but it was like she didn't even know what she had. "You can't take anything for granted. Life is way too short for that."

SEVENTEEN

Hailey continued to look out at the street, while Eric's mind washed with memories long buried. "I don't even remember my dad. He was serving ten years for armed robbery. Since he got out he's never once called me or Aaron. Our foster mom moved to Florida two years ago. I haven't seen or heard from her since, and before that I only got calls when she needed a new refrigerator or her washer quit working."

Old hurts boiled up inside him. "Maybe you should thank God every day that you have a dad who gave up the quiet years of his life to help you raise your daughter. He probably jumped at the chance to put a roof over your heads when you needed it most."

Hailey's head whipped around, her eyes dark. "I don't need you to educate me about my own father. I know exactly what he thinks of me."

"Yeah, he loves you."

Hailey laughed, but the sound held no humor. "Just because he didn't leave doesn't mean he actually wants to be around. You don't know anything about my father or his reaction to finding out his college-student daughter was pregnant."

Eric's stomach churned. He'd overstepped his bounds.

The last thing he wanted was to put something else between him and Hailey's trust, but he'd been so mad she had a father who was present and she was taking that for granted. "Hailey—"

"I won't ever forget the look on his face. Did you know he told me what happened was my fault, like Charles had nothing to do with it? After Kerry was born my dad didn't even look at her for a month. He just left me alone with a baby and Charles."

Hailey fisted her hands in her hair on either side of her face. "We were barely adults. We didn't know what we were doing. And all of a sudden there was this tiny person expecting the world from us." She sucked in a choppy breath. "Charles just checked out. For weeks at a time I barely saw him. But I didn't care. I had Kerry, and she needed me."

"Why did you marry him?"

"I didn't know what else to do. Charles was the only person who stood by me, even though it was barely anything. I still needed that if I was going to finish school and raise Kerry."

"I'm sorry."

Her eyes narrowed. "For what?"

He knew she didn't want his sympathy. "For overstepping. I shouldn't have gotten mad at you about your dad just because of mine. I apologize."

Hailey opened her mouth, but the sound of a boat approaching cut her off.

Two cops on a small police boat with a sputtering motor pulled up to the house. Hailey was glad she hadn't been allowed to say what she'd been meaning to. Her relationship with her dad was way too complicated, and Eric had never experienced anything like that. How did he think it was okay to have an opinion on something he barely knew anything about?

Hailey shoved away the thoughts and watched as the first cop stalked toward them, his eyes alert. She'd seen him around town but didn't know his name. Why did he seem to be more focused on Eric than on her?

Rain dripped off the edge of the plastic protecting his hat.

The partner brought up the rear, eyes hard as if this was an intense situation rather than taking over as babysitter of a body until the crime scene techs could arrive. This second guy was heavier-set, and older, with a belly honed by a steady diet of donuts.

They climbed the front steps slowly, ponchos billowing out around them like tents.

Hailey made a split-second decision. She stuck out her hip and said, "What's up, guys?"

The two police officers stopped on the porch, crowding her and Eric against the front door.

The first one up the stairs, with the plastic-covered hat, said, "I'm Banks. This is Melon." He motioned with his finger toward his bigger partner. "Some of our boys picked up your boss."

Ah. Hailey breathed a sigh of relief. Turner was in custody, and now they'd be able to start clearing all this up. Maybe they were acting tough and being short instead of polite because they'd known Phelps personally, and didn't like that he'd been killed by a marshal. Were they suspicious of all marshals, and not just Hailey and Eric?

She led them inside, and Eric stopped beside her. "Turner was brought in?"

Officer Banks gave him a short nod. "You're Hanning?"

"Yes. I take it you guys are here about the body." Eric

motioned to the stairs. "If you'll trade out with us, we'll be on our way. We're in the middle of a manhunt."

The cops removed their ponchos at the same time, like they'd practiced it that way. Hailey almost laughed, but then both men rested their hands on their weapons.

She backed up a step and collided with Eric. "Relax, guys. Tell us what's going on."

Banks shook his head. "Both of you need to stay where you are. We're to detain you until your people can get here."

Hailey frowned. "For what?"

Melon rocked to the balls of his feet and back to his heels. It was probably all the exercise he got in a week. "How would we know? We're only lowly police officers, not fancy-shmancy federal types."

"Does this have anything to do with Turner?"

Eric looked worried. Hailey was, too, but he was the one who'd been in the room when Turner shot Phelps. She didn't doubt he'd told the truth about the rest of it.

Banks grinned. "Worried?"

Eric started to speak, but Hailey cut him off. "Should he be?"

Banks's eyes shot to her. "This is none of your business, little girl."

Fire erupted in Hailey's middle. She needed to not lose her temper—again—with someone they were supposed to have a professional relationship with. But it just grated on her, time after time, that they thought since she was a girl they could treat her like a second-class cop. Were these guys on the team that had ambushed them at the airport?

"You know—"

Eric grabbed her shoulders and pulled her back. "If this is none of her business, then she should be free to go."

"Not likely." Banks sneered. "Both of you are to remain here."

"Then tell us what's going on. Unless you care to blindly follow orders without question, regardless of what's right and what's wrong."

Banks worked his jaw back and forth, clearly not happy with the insinuation. Hailey figured someone with that few brain cells should at least have the judgment to understand their limitations.

He huffed, eyes on Eric. "Word on the grapevine is that the boss claims you told him Phelps was armed, which led him to fire on Thomas. Everyone wants to talk to you now. Far as we're all concerned you're fair game for Phelps's shooting."

"I'm not the one who killed that man."

"Yeah," Banks sneered. "But you didn't stop it, either. Did you?"

"Turner is the one who said he had a gun."

Melon laughed. "Says you."

Hailey couldn't help but think the storm had made everyone crazy. These guys didn't even care that there was a dead man upstairs. They were too busy fighting for the honor of another man who had been killed. It was like they'd grasped the one reason they could find to take out their frustration on someone.

Too bad it had to be Eric.

Hailey stepped in front of her partner and squared her shoulders at the cops. "Back off."

Banks stepped forward. "Make me."

Hailey nearly rolled her eyes. It was like dealing with a bunch of junior high boys. "You're taking charge of this scene. The body is now officially yours. My partner and I are leaving."

Melon elbowed Banks aside and stuck his chubby fin-

ger in her face. Then he called her a name she hadn't been
called in years.

Eric shoved Melon back. "You don't call her that."

Too bad everyone in town thought it was true. Thanks
to some choice words that had once lit up the rumor mill,
everyone in town figured the consequences of Hailey's
teenage partying had finally caught up with her.

Would it never die?

Getting pregnant by her college boyfriend hadn't done
her any favors. It hadn't been intentional, but in the end
what was done was done, and the town didn't seem to be
able to look past her actions. They acted as though Charles
had no hand in it.

They had simply condemned her as the one at fault,
when she was only trying to deal with it and move on—to
live her life as a mom. She hadn't planned to be a mom as
early as it happened, but she wasn't going to do anything
but give Kerry her best.

Melon launched at Eric, but Banks held him back.
"Don't bother. Clearly she got to this one, too."

The two of them laughed, as though she were a spider
who had caught Eric in her web. They really thought she'd
done that? She hadn't forced Charles to marry her. It had
been a mutual decision. And Eric was his own man. He
was going to do exactly what he wanted.

This was why she didn't date. Men were too unpredict-
able. The people in town were going to think what they
wanted to think, regardless of what she did. The truth
didn't matter to them. Or the fact that she'd gone to work,
come home and taken care of her daughter and her father
for years now.

It was like they were all oblivious to anything but what
they'd made up in their own minds.

Hailey faced down Banks and Melon. "Good to know

if I hear that description of me being said around town, I'll know who started it. Thanks, guys. That was a delightful reminder of why I like the past to stay in the past." Hopefully the cops were smart enough to catch on to the sarcasm.

Eric folded his arms. "The body is upstairs."

Hailey nodded. They had to get out of there and find Farrell and Deirdre. That woman was up to her fancy shirt in this whole mess. The town needed to realize who was being dishonest in this situation, and who was simply trying to live their life and be the best mom and marshal they could be.

The two police officers trod up the stairs, but not before Melon glanced back and shot her a dirty look. Hailey turned to Eric, but didn't make eye contact. "Let's hit the road."

He trailed after her to the front door, where he wrapped his hand around her elbow. He gently tugged her around. "You okay?"

Hailey shook her head, her vision blurry. "Can we just go?"

She didn't want him to see. He needed to believe their words didn't affect her or he would start to coddle her like the other guys did.

Eric powered the boat back out of the neighborhood.

Hailey sat up front where he couldn't see her face and let the rain wash away her tears.

EIGHTEEN

The water was five feet deep. Eric pulled the boat up as close as he could to the law enforcement base of operations. Hailey jumped out and tethered it to a rail, and they trudged up the muddy hill to the warehouse. Formerly part of the now defunct mill, it had been turned over to emergency services for the duration of the flood.

When they walked in, the whole place was crazy with people running and yelling. The afternoon was waning and most of these folks had been up more than twenty-four hours now, though none of them showed it.

Eric's body wanted to succumb to the fatigue of getting no sleep the night before. Eventually he'd need to rest, but that time hadn't come yet.

"Jonah!" Hailey's yell cut across the crowd of officers and staff.

Their supervisor turned and pointed over to a group of girls that included Kerry huddled on a cot, giggling. Sitting together, leaning over an iPad, they could have been hanging out at a slumber party. Eric was glad the girl could shut out the specifics of what was going on and trust the adults around her to take care of the danger.

In one day she'd been nearly kidnapped and had a gun held to her head. Kerry might be fine right now, but the likelihood was that she'd feel the impact at some point.

Hailey strode over to her daughter.

Jonah stopped in front of Eric and planted his feet, something he'd probably perfected on court detail. "You okay?"

Eric nodded. His arm still hurt where the bullet had sliced his skin, but he wasn't going to bother anyone for a pain pill unless he really had to. Right now the discomfort was keeping him awake.

"Turner came in with two cops who'd been searching for residents stranded in their homes. I can't detain him on the basis of your word against his, and no judge would issue a warrant right now, especially when there's only your statement."

Eric bit back a wince. "Where's he now?"

"He went out with the sheriff to coordinate the transfer of some prisoners. A bus got washed out and tipped over so they took a team to lock it down and get them all on the road again. The sheriff isn't going to let Turner out of his sight. Not until all of this can be cleared up and we can get to the bottom of it. We need every able body right now."

Eric blinked. His tired brain was having trouble comprehending all that. Maybe he did need to take a rest.

Hailey wandered back over, frowning. She nudged his shoulder. "You okay?"

Eric ran his hand down his face. He must look rough if everyone was asking him that. "Yeah. How's Kerry?"

"She's having the time of her life." Hailey smiled. "Come on. Let's gas up before we head out again. That all right with you, Jonah?"

Jonah nodded, and Hailey pulled Eric over to the coffee station. Hailey poured two cups, grabbed half a dozen packets of sugar and ripped the tops off all at the same time. She split the stack in half and dumped the contents in their cups. Half of her attention was still on Kerry in the way that only a mom could pull off.

He glanced at Kerry and her posse of girls. She looked up like she'd felt her mom's attention on her, and gave him a hesitant smile and a little wave. Eric smiled and waved back.

Hailey handed over his cup and glanced where he'd been looking. Her face softened. "I should probably tell her what's happening. Charles is her father, and even since the divorce I've made a point not to say anything to take away from their relationship. Everyone should have two parents, if they can."

She was silent a moment, and then she said, "Jonah won't let her leave with anyone, so she's protected here. Should I tell her Charles might be involved?"

Eric didn't know about the two-parent thing, since he'd never had the chance to experience it himself, but he got what Hailey was saying. "I can see trying to protect her from the drama of the divorce. That's a good thing."

"And the hurt."

Eric glanced at Hailey and saw the pain she tried so hard to hide from everyone.

"She doesn't need to know that I cried when I found out I was pregnant because I didn't want a baby. I wasn't ready for a life other than the one I'd been so looking forward to. I had plans, you know? But then she kicked inside me, and I just melted. When I held her in my arms for the first time…there's nothing like that feeling. I tried to shield her from the horrible things people said about me. I'm sure she's heard them all, but I did my best not to be bothered by it."

"So you just buried it?"

Hailey shrugged. "And yet people still think they can hand over their opinion and I should just take it."

Eric's heart broke for all she kept hidden, just for the sake of her peace of mind.

"When I told him I was pregnant, my dad was so mad. All he said was how disappointed my mom would have been with my behavior." She paused. "Charles said he'd be there for us. He was already planning on going into politics. I guess he figured if anyone found out about us it would ruin his reputation. So we got married, and for the first few weeks we took turns watching Kerry and going to class. His parents weren't happy about it, but we were a team, or I thought we were. It worked for a while, at least."

"I'm glad you had him to help you."

Hailey gave him a small smile. "Me, too. We were friends once, despite what's happened since. It was after Kerry turned one that things started to derail. Charles had more classes, and he was working toward graduation—like I wasn't. He said he needed to focus." Hailey shrugged. Evidently the urge to vent over Charles's behavior had dissipated.

Eric gave her a squeeze. "For what it's worth, I'm proud of what you've made of your life."

Hailey blinked, and Eric wondered for a second if she was going to accept his compliment. But she pulled away from him and smiled, brushing it off. "How about you, what's your sob story?"

Eric chuckled. She was probably talking about him getting kicked out of WITSEC. Little did she know that his entire life was a continuing saga of sob stories, though there was one that surfaced above the rest. "I was engaged, once. It was a few years ago."

"Engaged?"

Eric nodded. "Sarah was on the street outside of the office where she worked, gunned down for no other reason than she'd stepped out of her office to go home for the day. A car drove by and opened fire."

He took a breath and gave himself a minute. Sarah could have died so easily. "She was paralyzed from the waist down, but she wouldn't let me see her or help her with anything. Her father told me she just wanted to be alone, but I kept coming back and coming back. She wouldn't even talk to me on the phone. Eventually I realized she wasn't going to let me in again."

"I'm so sorry." She looked like she wanted to say more, but she held back.

"I am, too. What's funny...well, it's not really funny, but I think I've realized it never would have worked. I liked the idea of her, I think, more than I loved who she was. She was the epitome of what I wanted in life. Beautiful, successful. But it made me feel like a fraud trying to match up to her."

Especially given the sorry state of his family growing up. The only person he'd ever been able to count on was his brother, Aaron. If the experience with Sarah had taught him anything, it was that no woman was ever going to think he was good enough. And he'd accepted that fact.

"You really think that?"

Eric shrugged. "I feel better being me. Even if who I am is the tubby twin who got beat up for being a nerd."

"Ugh." Hailey rolled her eyes. "Kids are so cliché."

Eric chuckled. "I've never thought of it like that. It didn't feel so cliché when they were pounding on me before my brother swooped in to save the day."

"He did that a lot?"

Eric thought about Aaron and how even now he was trying to make his way to town from the airport. "You have no idea."

Jonah strode over, his eyes on Hailey. "You two saddle up. I need you out there."

"What's going on?"

"Deirdre Phelps is at the high school. She says she knows where Farrell is, but she'll only talk to you." Jonah's gaze settled on Hailey.

Hailey downed the rest of her coffee and slammed the cup down on the table. "Let's roll."

Eric caught Jonah's eyes as she strode away and saw him grin. "Is she always like that?"

"Yes." Jonah laughed. "Take care of each other."

Eric nodded and went after his partner. The last day had been a tough mix of personal and professional drama for Hailey, and yet she'd pushed it aside and kept on rolling. Eric watched her kiss Kerry and give her a hug before she moved with him to the door. How did she compartmentalize her life like that?

Sarah's paralysis and her ultimate rejection of him had left Eric reeling in a way that it had taken him years to come back from. Even still he carried a shadow of the depression with him.

If Sarah hadn't wanted him when it counted, when she needed support the most, what made him think any other woman would feel different? It was tough not to believe there was something lacking in him. He didn't know how to sustain a long-term romantic relationship. Failure would be inevitable, and Sarah must have known that.

Back in the boat again, Hailey was glad the rain wasn't getting worse. But it was still pouring. She pulled up the collar of her raincoat and folded her arms against the chill in the air. When the sun went down, it was going to get a lot colder, which wouldn't help the rescue crews any.

"Any idea why Deirdre asked for you?"

Hailey turned to Eric at the back of the boat and shook her head. Farrell's brother was the man they'd shot at the airport. One of them was responsible for his death. But still, all they had so far was Harmer's body, and Farrell still at large. And Deirdre...who knew what was happening with her. Was Deirdre helping Farrell locate the stolen jewels?

"You said you knew her in high school?"

Hailey pulled the collar of her coat down. "In passing. We didn't exactly run in the same crowd."

He nodded, keeping his eyes on her until she looked away. Hailey's cheeks warmed from the attention. She couldn't let her feelings for Eric develop any further. He might have said it wouldn't have worked between him and the beautiful, successful Sarah, but Eric was the type of guy who would do anything for the woman he loved. He would have made it work, even if it meant giving up his whole life. She was sure of that.

Hailey had no intention of trying to live up to the perfect woman, even if part of her wanted to be reminded what it felt like to connect romantically with someone. Affection and the closeness that came with letting someone all the way into her heart...she'd known it in part with Charles. But however curious she was to know what being in love for real would feel like, she wasn't strong enough to risk losing the tight grip she had on her life.

Her sense of security lay in her badge and her gun. That was the way it was always going to be, regardless of her dad pestering her to let the pastor's words penetrate her heart. Hailey had to protect herself if she wanted to stay sane. She didn't know how to follow a God who might seem wonderful but still couldn't be fully understood. What if God asked more of her than she was prepared to give?

Hailey had heard people say again and again that God had done something they couldn't explain, or allowed something to happen and they didn't know why. That was fine for them if they wanted to trust in a God whose ways were "mysterious." She just wasn't going to let it happen to *her*.

The boat bumped the outer wall of the high school gymnasium, jogging Hailey from her thoughts.

"Whoa, sorry."

She looked back to catch Eric's grin as he fought to keep the boat straight in the rushing current of the river. Eric piloted the boat around the gym and got it as far as halfway up the steps to the main building. Hailey grabbed the rope and tied it to the railing.

She glanced at the walls of the buildings, then at the parking lot and the street out front. There was no one else around.

"I was expecting more of a welcome than this."

NINETEEN

Eric grabbed her hand and helped her jump from the boat to the top step. Hailey looked around. "Where are the cops who called it in?"

She pulled out her phone and dialed Jonah. There was no marking on the doors to indicate the building had been cleared. Someone would have painted or chalked an X, marking it off as empty and contained before they padlocked the door against looters.

It rang twice before Jonah answered. "Rivers."

Hailey launched straight in. "Where's Deirdre supposed to be? There are no cops here. There's nobody here at all."

"There should be two officers on scene."

Hailey hoped it wasn't the two from Harmer's house. The last thing she wanted was to run into those two sorry excuses for cops again. "Well, there isn't. This building hasn't even been cleared."

"I'll check what's going on. Proceed until I get back to you but use caution. Manpower is seriously limited and who knows what's going on. There could be people in there. But if Deirdre really is there, then we need her in custody."

Hailey heard the frustration in his voice. Apparently Jonah would be happy to give up his seniority for the sake of getting out there and facing this himself.

She unsnapped her gun holster. "Got it."

Eric did the same, drawing his weapon.

Hailey hung up. "Let's check the place out."

Eric led the way through the unlocked front doors. The flood was creating chaos all over town. The school and all of its equipment were open to anyone who wanted to come by and take whatever they wanted.

Looting was a sad fact of natural disasters, but since the local police and the sheriff had their hands full evacuating all the residents, it was hard to protect all the property as well. Still, someone should have been assigned to lock this building down.

The halls echoed as they walked, even with Hailey trying to keep her steps light. The whole place seemed eerily empty, especially since the lights were out. The power grid had been spotty all day. Hailey had figured when the whole town flooded the water would take out the electricity, too, but apparently it wasn't that cut-and-dried.

Hailey's phone vibrated in her pocket. She reached with her free hand, pulled it out and saw it was Jonah. "Shelder."

"Okay, this is weird. The cops are saying no one knows anything about the phone call from Deirdre. The guy who supposedly took the call is AWOL, and no one was ever sent to the high school to lock it down. You have no backup and this may or may not be a ruse."

"She's probably not even here. This is probably all a big joke." Maybe not likely, but possible—especially after a weekend full of attempted kidnappings, murders and secrets revealed that she'd had so far. "Should we check the whole school, just in case Deirdre is here?"

Jonah sighed over the line. Eric kept walking, so Hailey stayed beside him, glancing as he did into rooms as they walked. He might not be used to this work, but he knew what he was doing.

Jonah said, "This is the only lead we have. Whether or not it's a hoax doesn't make much difference. See it through, Shelder. But be careful. This could be a trap."

"Yes, sir." Hailey hung up and turned to Eric. "It's going to be a long afternoon."

Eric gave her a half smile. "It's already been a long day."

Hailey turned her attention back to the hall, rather than dwell on his smile. "A few more hours won't kill you."

Eric's chuckle filled the hall. They turned the corner and hit a stairwell. Two flights took them to another hall lined with lockers and classroom doors every thirty feet or so.

They checked out each one. She hadn't walked these halls in years, and it was horrifyingly familiar. Those days of bad hair and halfway decent grades were best forgotten. Whoever said the high school years were the best years of a person's life was crazy.

Hailey's experience was that things only got better as she'd grown older, especially now that Kerry was able to go running with her. Pretty soon she'd need to get Kerry down to the range and teach her how to shoot.

Blessed with being a lot more regular-looking than Hailey had in her teenage years, Kerry would probably breeze through the rest of her education relatively unscathed by bullies and "cool" kids trying to prove their own self-worth by humiliating everyone they thought was beneath them.

If Hailey were a praying kind of person, that would be the one thing she'd ask God for—that Kerry wouldn't be harmed, physically or emotionally. That school would just be school and not the nightmare Hailey had hated every minute of.

From Eric's earlier description of being beaten up for being a nerd, Hailey figured his teenage experience wasn't too different from hers—although he probably didn't have his name in the yearbook replaced with "The Hair."

There weren't many instances when Hailey mourned the loss of her mom more than those days, when some advice would have saved her a whole lot of teasing and heartache. She needed to get out of this building soon, or she'd start regressing into her teenage self.

Eric stopped. She heard a crackling sound and turned to him. His face was frozen and his body looked like every muscle had been locked tight with—

He dropped to the floor like a pile of books falling.

Beyond him stood Deirdre Phelps, the coils of her weapon embedded in Eric's back.

Hailey didn't have time to react before Deirdre lunged and sprayed something in her face.

Eric's hands were bound in front of him, and he was lying on a sticky linoleum floor. Deirdre must have caught him by surprise with the stun gun. Nothing else zapped through his body like that, locking up his muscles. He could still feel the buzz in his fingers, and his back stung where the two probes had pierced his jacket and embedded themselves in his skin.

Eric turned his head just enough to see Hailey, tied to a chair with Deirdre standing over her. Phelps had gotten the drop on his partner? Hailey's cheeks were red, her eyes were swollen and her nose was running.

Pepper spray.

It made sense. If Deirdre had used up her single stun gun shot on Eric she'd have needed a backup weapon.

Hailey looked at Deirdre, gritting her teeth together. Could she even see anything? "If I knew what you were talking about, I might take you up on that."

"Don't play coy with me. You know full well where we hid the stash. Farrell and I are going to get what's ours, and then we'll blow this backward town. So quit holding out on me and spill."

Farrell and Deirdre had stolen the jewels and hidden them?

Was Charles even involved?

Deirdre was the high-society daughter of a rich man. Why was she so interested in the jewels now?

Eric studied Hailey. Why did they think she knew where the jewels were?

Had she known it would come to this? Admittedly he didn't know much about his partner, but he'd been sure she was telling the truth. She'd claimed not to know anything about what Farrell and Deirdre were looking for. But Eric couldn't ignore the evidence. Deirdre looked pretty convinced Hailey knew where the jewels were.

Hailey lifted her chin. "Did Farrell tell you I know where it is? He probably sent you on this wild-goose chase so he could claim the stash all for himself."

"Just tell me where the jewels are."

"How should I know?"

Deirdre laughed, but the sound was like a hollow echo. "Maybe because of the large cash deposits your dad keeps using to pay for his medical treatment. That good enough for you?"

Hailey shook her head. "My dad isn't sick."

"Wow, you really think you can use the money for yourself, for your dad's medicines or whatever, and we wouldn't come after you?"

"Why do you need jewels, anyway? You have plenty of money."

Eric mentally cheered. They needed answers, and despite their disadvantaged position, this was the best way of getting information. Deirdre would hopefully be more inclined to talk if she thought she had the upper hand.

"I did. Until my dad cut me off, and told me to get a job. What is *that* about?" Deirdre huffed. "Farrell's brother told him about the money for your dad's treatment, and we knew you had to be fencing the jewels and using it to pay the old man's bills. Too bad for you, our score isn't your emergency fund."

Deirdre reached behind her and pulled out a handgun, holding it in her grip like she was familiar with the weapon. She lifted it and pointed it at Hailey's forehead. "Tell me where the rest of the jewels are."

Hailey swallowed.

Eric glanced around, scanning the area for a weapon. Deirdre had tied his hands behind his back, but if he could get up maybe he could tackle her hard enough to do some damage.

He'd probably get shot before he reached his feet, but Hailey needed the time to work out a plan of her own. All Eric had to do was create a diversion.

He couldn't completely count on Hailey having a plan in place, but he could guess. It's what he would expect. And there was a way to ensure whatever happened next had a chance of working.

God, we need Your help now. I know I haven't exactly talked much to You lately. Can You forgive me for that? I still don't like that You brought me here, but Hailey and I need You if we're going to get through this. I know that.

Deirdre's phone rang and she let the aim of her weapon slip while she swiped to answer the call. "She says she doesn't know anything about the money." Her lips curled up. "Got it." She pressed a button and held the phone out.

"We have eyes on that kid of yours." Farrell's brusque, scratchy voice came through the speaker. "And your old man. Now tell us where the jewels are, or your dad meets his demise earlier than the cancer had planned and your girl becomes an orphan."

An orphan? Did Farrell plan to kill Charles, too, or had he already done it? That was the second time some-one had mentioned cancer. Hailey looked sick, and Eric didn't know anything about it. Her dad hadn't confided that in him, but that didn't mean it was a lie. Eric studied her face. Did Hailey not know?

"Right now. Tell us or we kill them."

Hailey struggled against the bindings. "I don't know where the jewels are. But I can tell you this much. You harm one hair on either of their heads, and I'll kill both of you."

He saw a tear fall from the corner of her eye and his heart ached. The surge of protectiveness didn't surprise him. Eric knew his own feelings well enough to recall how it felt to care for a woman.

Keeping them from harm was where he failed. It was better to hold his heart separate, when it was only liable to get stomped on when she realized everything he was lack-ing. If Hailey was going to change her life and let someone in, it should be a better man than Eric.

"I don't know where it is." Hailey's voice was small, like all the pain she was feeling had subdued her.

He hated to see her like that.

Eric tucked his feet close to his body and started to slowly fold up to a standing position, praying Deirdre's focus would stay on Hailey and the phone.

Farrell's voice came through the speaker one more time. "Shoot her kneecaps."

Deirdre drew the phone back and ended the call with a shaky finger. Her face blanched. Didn't she have the stom-ach for how far she'd sunk into this business with Farrell?

Eric straightened his legs and breathed, slow and quiet. He only had one chance, or they would both be dead.

He rushed Deirdre. Her eyes widened with fear a split second before Eric bent over and rammed his shoulder into Deirdre's stomach. He heard the exhale of breath rush out of her lungs and they hit the floor in an awkward tangle of limbs.

The phone shattered. Eric had no idea where the gun was, and with his hands bound he had no way of getting it. Hailey kicked out with her legs, trying to hit Deirdre but coming up short because she was inches too far away from her. She cried out in frustration.

Eric tried to get the woman off him and managed to roll to the side. He swung his legs up and tried to pin her with a wrestling move. He didn't have many options. This was a plan with a lot of holes, but what kind of partner would he be if he didn't even try?

He got the angle wrong and managed to kick Deirdre in the head. She shook off the daze and moved to scrabble around for something.

Eric realized what she was going for at the same moment she lifted the gun and pointed it in his face.

"Don't move."

TWENTY

"Stop!" Hailey's breath came in pants. Her face was on fire, and she could barely see through her swollen eyes. She'd been sprayed with pepper spray during training, but it didn't make the sensation any more comfortable.

Deirdre turned back to Hailey. She had apparently recovered from her flash of panic at Farrell's order to shoot her in the kneecaps, because there was now a gleam of something sinister in Deirdre's eyes. "Where are the jewels?"

The gun pointed at Eric's face didn't move. Hailey wanted to scream. Why did they think she knew where the stupid things were? And what was all this about her dad having cancer? There was no way he could be sick. He'd been under the weather lately, but if it was worse than that she'd have known. Wouldn't she?

Hailey stared at Deirdre, but her thoughts went to Charles. Was he really involved with Farrell and Deirdre, and the theft of stolen jewels? She wanted to believe her judgment wasn't so warped as to have trusted a man who could be involved in something like this. But Hailey figured anything was possible at this point.

She forced herself to focus on Deirdre. "Don't hurt my partner."

After all, they needed to get out of this so she could ask her dad why he hadn't told her he was sick—maybe even dying.

Deirdre's eyes narrowed. "The jewels?"

Hailey lifted her chin. "Untie me, and I'll take you to them."

"Hailey, no!" Eric's gasp and shout were pretty believable, until she saw the quirk in the side of his mouth just for her. Good. He knew she was bluffing, and he was going to support her. The rush of emotion was unmistakable. Was this what a true partnership felt like?

Deirdre's head swung back and forth between them. "You two think you can keep the jewels for yourselves, do you? I don't think so."

Hailey held back from shaking her head. Deirdre really believed that? She really thought they were going to keep the jewels for themselves?

Deirdre reared back and kicked Eric in the stomach with her designer boot.

He coughed. "Was that really necessary?"

Hailey was ready to be done with this. "Untie me. Now."

Deirdre stepped closer, aiming her gun at Hailey. "You don't need your hands to walk."

"Fine." She would get free some other way. "Then help me up."

As soon as Deirdre was within range, Hailey did what she had been waiting for the chance to do. She bent her knees and kicked Deirdre's legs out from under her so she fell. Hailey shoved the gun away with her boot while Deirdre squealed and tried to get up.

Eric scrambled over and pressed his weight on Deirdre's torso to hold her down. Somehow they were going to have to get out of their bindings and get Deirdre restrained before they could bring her in. It was a shame they couldn't just leave her there, tied up in the school for someone else to pick up after the floodwaters washed away. She'd be fine for a couple of days.

Hailey shoved Deirdre's splayed leg toward the other one and sat on her knees. She glanced down at the disgruntled princess. "Word to the not-so-wise. You should have restrained my legs."

Deirdre squirmed. Eric looked up, his face flushed but happy. "So what now?"

Hailey laughed. "How should I know? I was the one who brought her down. Maybe you should be the one to figure out how we get out of these restraints."

Eric rolled his eyes. "Now you tell me."

Deirdre's voice was muffled, her face pressed against the floor.

Hailey leaned down. "What was that?"

She muttered another collection of choice words and shifted enough to lift her head. "Your kid dies if I don't call in. Let me up! Or do you want her dead? Maybe that'll make you realize we're serious. Steve Farrell won't be stopped. You can't best him, so get off me. And get off your high horse. You're no better than any of us."

Hailey shook her head and glanced at Eric. "How many times have I heard that today?"

Eric's face said he didn't think it was too funny. "I'm sorry. They shouldn't say stuff like that to you. It's not right." He shifted, causing Deirdre to cough and groan.

"Comes with the territory, Eric. It's a small town. People think they know you so they think they have the right to correct you if you're going wrong, or comment on your wayward ways."

"It's still not right."

"I know that." Hailey shrugged. "But it happens."

"Why not take Kerry and go somewhere people don't know you?"

"I like it here."

Eric laughed.

"I'm serious." Hailey smiled, liking the sound of Eric's laughter. It was rich and full, smooth like his voice. She could get used to hearing it way too easily.

Movement brought her attention to the door. Parker shook his head at the two of them sprawled on top of Deirdre. "What are you guys sitting around for?"

Hailey motioned him over with her head. "You got a knife?"

Parker looked offended. "I used to be with the SEALs. Are you really asking me if I have a knife?"

"Just cut us loose, will you?"

"Sure. In a second." Parker grabbed Deirdre's elbow and hauled her up, spilling Eric and Hailey onto the floor. He handcuffed her.

"How did you find us?"

Parker cut Hailey's bonds first. "Jonah said you might need some help."

He handed her a wad of tissue, and she wiped her nose. Hailey didn't waste any time before she dialed Kerry's number and stepped away from the two men. She needed to wash her face, because she still couldn't really see, but that could wait a minute.

"What's up, Mama?"

The tightness in Hailey's muscles eased. Kerry was safe, and Farrell had been bluffing. "Just checking in. How's everything?"

"It's *so* boring, Mom. When are you going to be *done*?" Kerry sighed, full of preteen drama. "Jonah wants to go out in the rain. Apparently everyone's moving somewhere safer, but he won't let me go home to Grandpa. He says I have to go with all the cops over to the Falcons' stadium."

"Then you should go. Stay with Jonah, okay?"

"Why? What's going on?"

Hailey pressed her lips together, trying to figure out how forthcoming she should be. "Just be careful. Stuff is crazy right now, and you don't want to get separated from Jonah."

"All right, Mom."

Hailey said good-bye and hung up.

Eric strode over, a washcloth in each hand and a bottle of water tucked in his elbow. She shut her eyes and held his elbow. He wiped Hailey's eyes with a soapy cloth, poured water over her face to rinse it off—as if she wasn't wet enough from the rain—and then gave her the dry cloth.

Hailey patted her face and then lowered the towel. "Thanks."

His eyes surveyed her, the blue depths tempting her to get lost in his gaze, as though maybe if she fell deep enough she would discover something there. Parker cleared his throat. She looked and saw him smirking. Great.

Hailey snapped out of it, still feeling the residual warmth, and looked again at Eric.

A shuttered look had fallen over his eyes, and his lips were pressed into a thin line. "Deirdre says Kerry and your father will die if she doesn't call Farrell and check in."

Hailey wanted to stare more at his mouth, but there was no way she was going to let this go. She leaned past her partner to yell at Deirdre. "You suddenly decide to grow a conscience now? You were threatening me with their deaths a few minutes ago. More likely you're trying to save your own hide. Because my daughter and my father are *fine*."

Deirdre's face twisted with rage. "He'll come after me, too! If I don't get the jewels he'll kill me."

"That's what I thought."

Deirdre was trying to save herself. Hailey wanted to get in the boat and get to Kerry, even though she'd just spoken to her. She didn't want to go back out and continue the search for Farrell.

She called her dad to check in but didn't get an answer. She needed to make sure everything was all right there, too. If her dad was sick, he would need to rest, rather than spend hour after hour taking care of a horde of other people.

Eric glanced between her and Parker. "What if she calls Farrell and pretends to check in? Deirdre could get us Farrell's location."

"Help you?" Deirdre shook her head. "No way. Farrell will kill me for sure."

Deirdre didn't look happy, still handcuffed, sitting at the conference table in the office. Parker was on the phone in the main office, and Hailey had disappeared to wash up some more. Eric perched on the edge of the table, waiting for his answer.

When the floodwaters receded, Farrell and Deirdre were both locked up and the danger had passed, Eric was going to find a hotel room with one of those huge corner tubs and sit in it until the water went cold. Then he'd be clean.

His phone buzzed.

"Hanning." Eric answered with his eyes on Deirdre, who was looking away at the wall.

"Dude, what is going on?"

Eric's lips twitched. Aaron sounded miserable. "You tell me."

"It's a complete nightmare out here. How are you surviving? Are you okay? Are you really still working?"

He stilled. "Aaron, where are you?"

"At the Falcons' stadium. The sheriff says a team of marshals stayed behind to work. Are you crazy?"

Eric laughed. "You mean as crazy as you?"

"Hey." Aaron was laughing. "I resemble that remark."

As a former Delta Force soldier, Aaron had pulled one crazy stunt after another. Even when they were kids, Aaron was the one doing tricks on his bike, jumping ramps and breaking bones. Nearly every summer Aaron had been in a cast for some injury.

Soon Aaron would have nothing to worry about but dirty diapers.

He quit laughing. "Seriously, Eric, when are you going to get to safety?"

Eric couldn't answer that. He felt pretty safe. Or he would, when Hailey got out of the bathroom and came back in. Something about being in the same room with her made Eric feel better. He didn't think he needed to be physically safe to make things right, so long as whatever they were doing, they were doing it together.

"Okay, brother." Aaron laughed again. "What is her name? I thought you were chasing some escaped criminal?"

"We are."

"But…"

Eric sighed. "Her name is Hailey. She's my partner."

"And?"

Eric pressed his lips together. "And nothing. She's my partner, that's all."

He wasn't going to say much more with Deirdre listening. Eric didn't need his personal information being spread around everywhere. Given the surprise on Hailey's face

when he'd given her that quick kiss at his apartment earlier, she wasn't even thinking about him on the same terms.

"Listen, I've got to go."

"Okay, brother. Get to safety as soon as you can. And
if I can get there I'll come help you."

"You don't need to do that, Aaron."

"Yes, I do."

"I don't need your help, and I haven't for a long time."

Aaron tutted. "I've heard this refrain before."

"So why do you keep bringing it up?"

"Because I'm your big brother. If you're in trouble I'm
going to be there."

"I'm not sure two whole minutes counts all that much,
brother."

Hailey came into the conference room. Eric gave her a
small smile and thought of something. "Actually, I do have
a job for you. Look for Deputy Marshal Jonah Rivers. He's
with a twelve-year-old girl who has red hair and freckles.
Her name is Kerry. She's Hailey's daughter."

"The woman you're with has a *child?*"

Eric gritted his teeth. "Just find Kerry and make sure
she's safe. Tell her you're my brother. Show her that picture in your wallet."

Aaron laughed. "I sure will."

It would prove to Kerry that the two of them were brothers, at least. Eric hung up and put his phone back in his
pocket.

"Who was that?"

Hailey stood across the table, where he could talk to her
and she could keep Deirdre in view at the same time. She
was a smart, observant woman who loved fiercely. Who
couldn't appreciate that? "That was my brother, Aaron.
Again."

"The one on his way?"

Eric nodded. "He's at the stadium."

"And you told him to watch out for Kerry? Thanks."

"Of course." Eric knew what it would do to Hailey if something happened to her daughter.

Hailey turned to Deirdre. "So what's it going to be?"

Deirdre looked at them, her eyes deadpan. "Do I get my deal?"

Parker strode in. "The US Attorney does not like to be woken up in the middle of the night, especially when he's due at the golf course at six in the morning. So I'm surprised, but he says yes."

Hailey folded her arms. "What do you say, Deirdre?"

TWENTY-ONE

This was the part of their job he didn't like, the fact that criminals who deserved to be in jail so often got a free pass for the sake of shared information. He much preferred when they were given a new identity and still had to serve out some of their sentence. Guys like Farrell, who preyed on innocent people, didn't deserve to go free.

Deirdre set her handcuffed hands on the table and folded her fingers together. "Fine. Get me a phone, and I'll tell Farrell whatever you want. But if it doesn't work, it's not my fault."

Hailey leaned in. "If it doesn't work, any deal we offer gets accidentally shredded. So you do everything, and I mean *everything* to sell this, because if my child gets hurt because of you I will hunt you to the ends of the earth."

Eric believed her. Hailey wasn't going to risk Kerry being hurt. But it did feel like she might be taking her role as a mom too far. Not that he knew enough to be an expert on parenting. Who did? But if she trusted God to keep Kerry safe, wouldn't that be better? Bad things happened to everyone, but God was constant and faithful.

But for some reason, Eric doubted Hailey would welcome him telling her that. And saying it also meant Eric would have to take his own advice.

When was the last time he'd let God take control of his life?

Eric had made his own way through WITSEC and when it had fallen apart, he'd blamed God. In his selfishness, he hadn't wanted to let go of what he thought was his right— the career he loved. In reality, all he had a right to was whatever God chose to give him. And maybe, all this time, God had been leading him *here.*

To Hailey.

While Hailey talked with Deirdre about the details and Parker made notes, Eric bowed his head and prayed. When he opened his eyes, Hailey was looking at him curiously. He gave her a small smile.

She nodded. "I'm not letting Farrell get away with this."

"Deirdre will get us what we need, won't you?" Eric studied the woman, not entirely convinced this wouldn't end in a bigger mess than they were in already.

Deirdre made a convincing case, but Eric wasn't sure Farrell bought it. It would have to do, though. They were running out of options fast. Farrell might hold back from hurting Hailey's family, but he was still in the wind…or the rain, as the case was.

They left Parker to transport Deirdre out of town, and Hailey walked with Eric to the stairs. "You look exhausted."

Hailey laughed. "Thanks. You look like wet laundry yourself."

Eric wrapped an arm around her shoulders and squeezed. Hailey looked up at him, eyes wide at the comforting touch. But Eric didn't much care this was a work situation. He studied her face. "Why so surprised?"

"I'm just not used to it, I guess. Do you… I mean…"

"Am I interested in you?" Eric figured at this point he could very well be halfway in love with her, but she didn't need to know his feelings ran that deep. Not yet, at least. Especially given he'd so far only entertained the thought enough to quickly pray about it.

Hailey bit her lip and nodded.

"Yes. For the record, I am interested in you."

Hailey relaxed against him. "Me, too."

Eric turned her toward him, slid his arm around her waist and tilted her face toward his. He leaned in, put his cheek against her temple. He held her there with his lips against her damp hair while he rubbed his hand up and down her back.

"I could fall asleep like this."

Eric shook with laughter. "I might be offended if I didn't feel the same way." He pulled away and squeezed the back of his neck. "So where to now?"

Hailey pulled out her phone and studied it. "You know what's been bothering me for a while about this whole thing?"

Eric shook his head. "What?"

"Charles."

"You think he's involved?"

"I think he's the one who knows where the jewels are."

When they got to Charles's home they discovered the whole first floor was under water. Night was falling, bringing with it a chill that froze Hailey to her core. If she didn't get dry soon, she was going to get sick. Although, she was still plenty warm from Eric hugging her.

Eric piloted the boat to the nearest window. Hailey pulled out her phone and saw a missed call from her dad. Why hadn't he told her he was sick? Surely it wasn't as bad as Deirdre had made it out to be. If there really was something seriously wrong with him, she would know. Right?

The land line at her house rang and rang, and finally

someone picked up. "Yeah?" It wasn't her dad. This guy sounded young and obtuse.

"Put Alan Shelder on the phone."

"Don't know where he is."

"Well, go find him."

"He ain't here."

Hailey sighed. "I appreciate this has probably been a trying day for you, but I am looking for my possibly extremely sick father—"

"Possibly?"

"Don't interrupt me. I need you to locate my father and have him call me."

"You ain't gonna come check on him yourself?"

Hailey helped steady the boat against the side of the house. The whole place was dark. Charles probably wasn't even here.

"I'm a little busy catching a wanted criminal, thank you very much." She didn't need a stranger to remind her that she neglected her father. She was well aware of that fact already. And if her dad hadn't volunteered the farmhouse as a safe spot for residents, she would have been there instead of dragging Kerry to the warehouse.

But that was how their relationship had always gone. Coexisting, but never really connecting. "Just have him call me."

Hailey hung up and stowed the phone in her inside jacket pocket. If it came into contact with much more water the thing was going to stop working altogether. It would be a fitting end to this weekend if she had a broken phone on top of everything else that had been damaged.

She looked out over the town. Gray clouds streaked the night, blocking the determined rays of sun trying their best to light the sky. Too bad it was a losing battle. Kind

of like Hailey's life. The water was rising. Would they all
be swept away like debris?

Eric used his flashlight to break a pane of the window
and punched out as many of the jagged edges around the
frame as he could. He crawled in and Hailey followed.

She stopped and looked at what was her daughter's bedroom in her ex-husband's house. She'd been in here before,
picking up Kerry to bring her home. It was still weird that
her daughter had a bedroom in someone else's house. It
had to be hard on her to have two homes, two parents who
lived separate lives. It wasn't anywhere near ideal, but it
was how Kerry's life had turned out.

She could feel Eric's warmth beside her, but she didn't
turn around. The rush of emotion she felt for him was
more than she could deal with. Hailey pulled out her phone
again, needing to connect with her daughter.

Jonah picked up straight away.

"How is she?"

There was a pause, and Hailey heard movement, then
Jonah said, "Talking with her friends still." He barked out
a low laugh. "Who knew there was so much to say? Whatever it is, it's apparently deathly important."

Hailey chuckled. "When you're that age, everything
is. Has she eaten?"

"I gave her a sandwich. She didn't seem impressed,
but she ate it."

"Thanks, Jonah."

"No problem. We'll be moving out shortly. I'll keep
her with me."

Hailey thought of Eric's brother. "If you run into an
Aaron Hanning, he's Eric's brother, and he's going to keep
an eye out for Kerry if you need it."

"Got it. I'm still not going to let her out of my sight."

Hailey figured there was something underneath the surface that drove Jonah to be so protective of Kerry. It was like he'd seen the worst of what could happen when an innocent was left alone and defenseless. Hailey knew. She'd gone through it herself.

"Thanks, Jonah." It didn't quite convey the gratitude she felt, but if she got mushy he'd just brush it off. "I'm trusting you with everything I have."

"I know that, Hailey. She'll be fine."

Hailey hung up

If she got married, it wouldn't necessarily make things better for Kerry. It might even bring a whole new set of problems to their lives, even if she didn't think Eric would be like that. He seemed pretty straightforward, but how was Hailey supposed to know? And why on earth was she considering marriage to him anyway? What was *that* about?

Eric's brow twitched. "What?"

Hailey shook her head. "Let's go find Charles and get some answers."

The hall was empty. Water would be halfway up the stairs by now, but Hailey checked anyway. Charles lay half in and half out of the water, which was tinged with red. He'd been beaten. Badly.

Hailey rushed to his side, and Eric helped her haul him out of the water to the landing at the top of the stairs. They laid him on the carpet and he moaned.

"Charles, can you hear me?"

"Hailey?" His eyes flickered open. "I thought I was going to die."

"Who did this?"

Charles winced. "Farrell."

Eric looked at his watch. "How long ago was he here?"

"Hours, maybe." Charles breathed. "I don't know."

"Where's Beth-Ann?"

"Gone."

Right. Hailey might not get on with Charles most of the time, but she didn't like that his wife had left him alone to deal with everything by himself.

"Aren't you supposed to be evacuating like everyone else?"

Charles grunted and tried to sit up. Hailey didn't figure it was a good idea, but she helped him anyway, knowing he'd deal with the pain for the sake of not looking weak.

Charles leaned his head back against the wall and closed his eyes. "I was checking on one last thing and got caught here. The water swept my car away, so I figured I'd go upstairs when it got too high. Then Farrell came. I barely made it up the stairs, or I'd have drowned."

Eric crouched beside Charles. "What did he want?"

His eyes moved to Hailey instead. "Looking for the jewels. Looking for you."

Hailey fought down the rising anger. Getting mad at him always made him shut down even more. She tried to keep her voice as even as possible when she said, "Charles, why do Farrell and Deirdre think I know where the jewels are?"

TWENTY-TWO

Hailey could feel Eric's eyes on her, but she needed to know the truth so badly she didn't break the eye contact between her and Charles.

"Hail—"

"You sold me out."

Charles sucked in a choppy breath. But she knew better than to think it was due to regret and not to bruised ribs. Hailey wanted to fly off the handle. Put her fist through the drywall. Kick something.

"Why." It wasn't a question. He was going to tell her.

His eyes darkened with what might have been actual regret. "I know you won't ever be able to forgive me and I don't blame you."

Had he ever cared about her at all?

She couldn't say it was okay, because there was no way it would ever be. But could she forgive him? The betrayal cut deep. She'd trusted Charles with the life of her daughter and he'd brought a criminal into their world.

Hailey drew in a deep breath. "I am going to try, but only because if I'm chewed up with hatred for you, Kerry will know. And no kid needs that between their parents."

A tear fell from the corner of Charles's eye, down his

cheek. "You're a better person than I am. You always have been."

Hailey didn't know about that. "Did you give my father money?"

Charles nodded. "He didn't want anyone to know."

"Know what?"

"About the cancer."

Hailey's gut twisted. "So it's true?"

"It's not terminal. He has a good chance of beating it, but it's taking its toll and his insurance won't cover everything."

"Why didn't he tell me?"

Charles grabbed her hand and squeezed. "He didn't want you to worry."

Hailey wanted to laugh, but she was too frustrated.

"Yeah." Charles's lips lifted in what could have been a smile. "I told him that sounded like someone else I know."

She shook her head. "So whose jewels are they? Who did you and Farrell and Deirdre steal them from?"

Charles looked away, but Eric didn't much care if the man felt guilty. His actions had caused Hailey supreme heartache, and changed the course of their family's life. If only people could see what the consequences of their actions would be. Too bad it didn't work like that.

Hailey's grace astounded him. Eric wanted to pummel the man, to hurt him even more than Farrell already had for putting Hailey and Kerry in danger just to save himself. The strength of his anger surprised him, but then Hailey brought out that intense need to make sure nobody hurt her. Ever.

She'd been through enough, and was ready to promise he'd never let anything else happen to her. But how could he guarantee that? Sarah had been paralyzed. As much as he wanted to tell Hailey their future together would be fine, he couldn't assure her of that.

Hailey shook Charles's shoulder. "Who did you steal from?"

Charles's voice was low when he spoke. "Old Lady Mansion."

Hailey gasped. "You didn't."

"She was dying! It wasn't like she needed all those jewels. No one ever missed them. No one was going to come looking for their inheritance."

"So you conned an old lady out of her precious gems and you don't even care?"

Charles's face was red. "I didn't know they were going to kill her! I thought we'd sneak in and grab them while she wasn't looking. But Farrell went into her room. It was horrible. He—" Charles's voice broke and he hung his head, sobbing.

Eric couldn't believe what he was hearing. Teenage kids were just as capable of violence as adults. But he hadn't expected Hailey's ex-husband to be wrapped up with Farrell and Deirdre, the theft of jewels and the murder of an old woman.

Hailey's voice was flat. "And you used the money to buy yourself this life?"

Eric saw the vein in her neck pulse. He hauled her to her feet, pulling her back from Charles. "Take it easy, okay? He isn't in any condition to do this now. He needs medical attention."

"He should have thought of that before he robbed Old Lady Mansion. He's an accessory to murder."

Charles yelled, "I wasn't in the room. I was taking the jewels. I had nothing to do with killing her, that was all Farrell."

"Which makes you an accessory."

Eric touched her shoulder. "Hailey—"

"No." She brushed off his hand. "He doesn't even get it. He just confessed. He could go to jail."

"I know." Eric tugged her back. "We need to get him medical help."

"What's the point?" Charles cried. "You should leave me here to die."

"Seriously?" Hailey flung her arms up, nearly hitting Eric in the face. "You're just going to give up *now*? Kerry needs her father, and all you can worry about is yourself."

Charles's face twisted with pain. "You think I want to leave her? She's the best thing I ever did. But if what you say is true, she shouldn't have to live with her father being in jail for murder."

"Let's just call Farrell, then." Hailey slammed her hands on her hips. "He can come back and finish you off. After all, what reason is there to live?"

Okay, this was getting out of hand. Eric strode over to Charles and hauled the man up. "Let's go."

He walked Charles past Hailey, who was grinning now she'd won the fight. Eric didn't mind helping her, but not when that meant he was the referee between them. Especially considering the fact they clearly had a lot they needed to talk about.

Eric glanced between them. "Have you guys thought about counseling?"

Hailey's smile dropped from her face, leaving a grimace. "We're not a couple anymore."

"I know that. But it doesn't mean you don't have stuff that needs to be said."

Charles let out a huff, which if he wasn't injured might have been laughter. Eric continued through Kerry's room to the open window.

"Charles?" At Hailey's question, Eric turned them both back. "Where are the jewels now?"

Eric waited for him to answer.

"Where did you put them?"

Charles looked at the floor, then up at Hailey again. "They're long gone."

Hailey looked like she could spit fire. Eric thought that if he stared enough, he'd be able to see the flames in her eyes. "How much was there?"

"Two-point-two million."

"How could you?" Hailey's voice was hollow.

"You didn't seem to mind too much when it was keeping you in a life of luxury."

"You really think I cared about that?"

"It's not like you ever went anywhere. I thought you were basking in it. Living the life."

Hailey grimaced. "I couldn't go anywhere, because I couldn't stand to hear what everyone was saying about me."

Eric glanced between them, wondering how a couple could be married and still have so much that had gone unsaid. He prayed it wouldn't have been like that with him and Sarah, but it easily could've been. Hailey had been trying to protect herself and her new baby, and Charles had been trying to assuage his guilt over the theft and pretend he hadn't done something awful.

Eric turned to him. "Why didn't Farrell and Deirdre realize you had taken the jewels?"

Charles kept his eyes down. "There were so many and we agreed to hide them all until everyone forgot about what had happened. At first I didn't think they'd care about a few here or there. Then Farrell went down for assault the first time. I thought he'd be out of my hair forever. He wouldn't have had any way of knowing the jewels were gone, so I started paying off my mortgage a little at a time."

Eric said, "And then?"

"One day I went to get more and I realized nearly two-thirds of what we'd originally taken was gone. That was when I stopped. I saved it, until Alan came to me about his medical bills."

Hailey opened her mouth to say something, but her phone rang. She turned away to answer it, and Eric looked at Charles. The man's attention was on him, like he was trying to figure out who Eric was and why he was here with Hailey.

"Are you her boyfriend?"

"I'm not sure that's any business of yours."

Charles's lip curled. "We have a child together."

"I'm aware of that." Eric folded his arms. "And you might have a role in each other's lives, but that doesn't mean you get a say in what Hailey does with her personal time."

Charles uttered some choice words and came at Eric like he was looking for a fight.

"Don't."

It shouldn't have pleased Eric to have so much power over Charles, especially when the man was barely holding himself upright. He'd never abused his position before, but Charles didn't know that. Eric needed to get a handle on his anger before his protective side got him in trouble.

Charles looked down his nose despite the fact Eric was taller. "So you're going to swoop in and be her hero?"

Gone was the guilt and shame of what Charles had done. It was like the man didn't even remember their conversation from only minutes ago. Now his face held all the obstinacy of a rich man in a position of power who thought he was the only one who had a say over Hailey's life. Like no one else should be allowed near her.

Eric was going to have to get through a lot of hoops if he pursued Hailey for real. Which made him wonder how many men over the years had shown an interest in Hailey and been warned away or scared off by her ex-husband?

Good thing Eric's determination was strong enough to go head-to-head with Charles's pride.

Eric said, "What is or isn't between Hailey and I isn't any business of yours."

A gleam flashed in Charles's eyes. "So you're not together."

Not yet. Then again, maybe being goaded into competing for Hailey's affection wasn't the best motive for telling her how he felt. Eric shook his head. "It's seriously none of your business."

"What—" It was the shake in Hailey's voice that made Eric whip his head around to look at her.

Hailey's eyes were hard. "I want proof of life."

TWENTY-THREE

"Mom?" Kerry's voice shook like she was crying.

Hailey gripped the phone. "Baby, what's—"

"I told you I had my eyes on her. Now I have your daughter." It was Farrell. "Bring me my jewels or I'll kill her."

"What?" Hailey's stomach dropped. Kerry was supposed to be with Jonah. What was she doing with Farrell? Why hadn't her team leader kept her daughter safe like he'd said he would?

Eric was suddenly beside her, squeezing her shoulder. She looked up and saw the question in his eyes, but her mouth wouldn't work.

"You have one hour to get the jewels and meet me at the church on Pine and Fortnam. Come alone. No tagalongs, no other cops, no funny stuff. Now get me my jewels."

"And if I don't have them?"

"You'd better pray you find them, or the kid is dead."

The line went silent.

Hailey wanted to throw the phone. Before Eric could say anything, she told him what Farrell had said.

Charles whimpered, and both of them turned to him. "He has my daughter?"

Hailey strode over to her ex-husband. "Are there any jewels left that you know of?"

"You're going to get her back?"

Hailey looked at the ceiling and then back at Charles. "Of course I'm going to get her back. What do you think? But I have to give Farrell something or he'll kill her, Charles. He's going to murder *my* daughter because of your stupid actions."

Charles sputtered. "It's not…I don't…"

"This isn't getting us anywhere." Eric came to stand alongside both of them.

"Eric is right." Hailey kept her eyes on Charles. "If we don't give Farrell something, Kerry will be dead."

Charles's face bled of color, leaving it a pasty gray she'd only seen when he'd had a stomach bug.

Eric folded his arms. "What about your wife?"

Hailey shot Eric a glance. Now who was wasting time?

Charles shook his head. "What about her?"

"Does she have any jewelry? At least something we can use as a decoy?"

Hailey didn't think much of Eric's idea. "What do you mean 'we'? He said come alone."

Eric waved away her concern. "I'm not letting you go alone."

Hailey said, "But you have to take Charles in, and find out what happened to Jonah."

"Well then, there's no time to waste."

"She gets like that when she's freaked out," Charles said. "The more scared she is, the more she talks."

"I do not."

Eric looked at her with warmth and compassion.

Hailey couldn't let herself accept it, not now. "Are we all just going to stand here while Farrell has my daughter?"

Eric turned to Charles. "Where's your safe?"

The two men left the room and Hailey heard the beeping of a keypad. She'd seen the jewelry Beth-Ann wore enough to know where a chunk of the original jewelry money had gone.

Charles must've had a hard time going out of his way to fence the pieces for cash. Hailey wondered how she could have missed it. But then she'd been seriously distracted by her new baby, and hadn't thought much of Charles's absences. In truth, she hadn't wanted to be around anyone back then.

The thought of Charles having been involved made her sick. Though not as sick as she felt knowing Farrell had Kerry in his clutches. She called Jonah, wanting to know what had happened. The phone rang and then went to voice mail. Her hand shook, and she dropped her phone.

Hailey bent over and sucked in air. She needed her daughter back, safe in her arms. She couldn't believe Jonah would let her go with Farrell without something serious happening. Was he dead?

She squeezed her eyes shut and prayed. She hated that it had to come to this before she admitted she needed help, but she'd been stubborn.

A warm hand touched her back. She grabbed her phone and straightened. Eric left his palm there, and rubbed his firm hand up and down her spine just like he'd done at the office. Once again, Hailey's tension eased just enough for her to re-group.

"I'm okay."

Eric frowned. "I wouldn't be."

Hailey studied his face. He looked as worried as she felt, which might not be good if one of them needed to be emotionally clearheaded. "We don't have much time to get across town."

Eric touched her cheek, and then slid his hand back so

his fingers were in her hair. Hailey's ponytail had fallen out hours ago, and she figured the rain had made her hair a ball of frizz. Eric didn't seem to care. He looked like he wanted to reassure her that he was going to take care of everything, but wasn't able to promise her that.

He touched his lips to hers, much the same as he'd done in his apartment. But this time she was prepared for the rush of warmth and the feeling of comfort. Just when Hailey was going to pull back and tell him they needed to leave, he saved her the trouble.

"We should go now."

She nodded. Charles stood just behind Eric, his hands now uncuffed and holding a lumpy velvet bag. She headed for the window and the men followed behind. Hailey thought she heard Charles mutter, "I knew you were her boyfriend," but she couldn't be sure.

When this was over, things were going to go back to normal. Kerry would be safe, and Hailey would no longer need anyone else in her life. Eric was nice enough to help her now, given this was a stressful situation, but that didn't mean anything was going to come of it. It was just him being comforting.

Eric drove the boat through town once again. Night had fallen while they were in Charles's house, and she wondered if Kerry still had her coat. Was her daughter dry and warm? Hailey was going to get her away from Farrell, whatever the cost, but there were some things she couldn't protect Kerry from.

After what seemed like forever they finally reached the church. Hailey hadn't attended services in weeks. She offered God an apology, hoping He didn't mind her being brief, and then tacked on a quick request for Kerry to be safe. It wasn't ideal, but she could rectify that later.

Eric climbed out of the boat, took the bag of jewels from

Charles and handed it to her. "I'll take the back door and only step in if you need me, okay?"

Hailey nodded, and Eric pointed at Charles. "You stay here."

"Yes, sir."

Hailey didn't look back at her ex-husband. He was going to be belligerent even if it cost them everything.

She kept her focus on Eric. "Stay safe."

"You, too."

Hailey sucked in a breath, drew her weapon and walked into the church. Kerry was sitting in the front row of chairs. She jerked around and saw Hailey. "Mom!"

Farrell was nowhere to be seen.

"Kerry, let's go!"

Kerry's face fell. "Mom, look out—"

She turned in time to see Farrell rush at her, but he was coming too fast. Too fast for her to get a shot off. Hailey swung the gun and caught Farrell in the temple.

"Go, Kerry!"

He didn't stop, but barreled into her at full speed. They hit the floor, and for a second Hailey couldn't breathe. She squirmed and tried to hit him, but he slammed her gun hand against the tile floor again and again.

Hailey cried out. Where was Eric? She couldn't move, couldn't breathe. She wanted to throw up, but all she could do was ignore the screaming pain in her hand and keep fighting him.

She wasn't a scared young woman with a new baby anymore. She was a federal agent with a gun and a partner. "You're under arrest, Farrell!"

He laughed. "Nice try."

The gun fell from her hand and slid across the floor. She grabbed Farrell to keep him from getting it, and hit him with her left hand instead. The pain in her right hand was blinding—surely all the bones were broken.

Farrell's face was awash with rage as he grappled with her, now trying to get a grip on her neck. She didn't know how long she was going to last before the pain made her lose consciousness.

It figured her partner would let her down at a time like this. Hailey should have known Eric wasn't any more trustworthy than any of the other men in her life.

If she was going to get her and Kerry out of this, she was going to have to do it herself.

Eric finally got over the mass of debris bunched against the side of the church. The dam had been at overflowing all day. He wouldn't be surprised if it failed completely and the whole town ended up underwater. It would take weeks, if not months, and millions of dollars, to get everything back to normal. An event like this was catastrophic, especially to small towns like this one.

So many people would be distraught if generations of history were destroyed by the water. Eric couldn't imagine what it felt like to have that kind of a connection to a place, but could admit—at least to himself—that he wouldn't mind having it with Hailey and Kerry. Even if it was here in this town.

The back door was in sight when gunshots rang out. It flew open and Kerry ran out, tripped and fell face-first into the water.

Eric waded through the knee-deep river that was rising fast to get to her. Kerry lay facedown. He lifted her out, water draining off her face as she spluttered and coughed.

"You okay?"

Her eyes were wide and bright. She was in shock. "Mom."

Eric lifted her by the elbows and set her beside the door,

out of sight. He had no way to get her safe or dry, not without leaving his partner. "Stay here."

He drew his weapon and swept down the dim corridor to the sanctuary. He didn't like leaving Kerry, but his partner needed help.

He was torn between two things. What won out was the fact Hailey and Kerry needed each other. They were both wet and cold, but he could make it so they were at least together.

His heart raced, his palms slick and his stomach roiling at the thought that something might happen to either of them.

Eric cleared the room. He was way too upset for someone who wasn't supposed to care about Hailey. But he did, he cared deeply. Still, simply because he was attracted to Hailey didn't mean she needed him.

It was dim and quiet in the corridor, but he heard movement. Was Farrell here, or gone?

Shuffling.

Eric stepped into view. His partner was grappling with Farrell, fighting for her life.

Hailey batted his hands away. Someone lifted Farrell up, out of her grasp.

Eric tossed the man to the side like he weighed nothing. The look on his face made her wonder why she didn't feel a little intimidated by her partner. He was capable of doing serious damage if the occasion called for it.

He paused a minute to haul her to her feet and then didn't let go of her hand. "Okay?"

Hailey nodded. "Nice timing."

"Gun?" He had his out.

Hailey cradled her damaged hand against her stomach and looked around. "It slid across the floor somewhere." Not that the thing would do her much good now. She wouldn't even be able to hold it.

"Mom?" Kerry stood by the rear door, her face pale. While Farrell shook off his daze, Hailey ran to her daughter and took her in her arms.

"It's okay, everything's okay." Hailey said it as much for her own benefit as for her daughter's. She turned and put Kerry behind her, searching for a way out.

Farrell was up and rummaging through the bag of jewels. He roared and dumped the bag out. The ruse was up.

Eric stood his ground, aiming his gun at the escapee. "It's over, Farrell."

Hailey pushed Kerry toward the front door, walking with her to make sure she got out this time. "Go sit with your father."

"No." Kerry spoke over her shoulder. "I don't want to leave you."

Hailey shoved her forward with one hand and turned back to Farrell.

"Farrell, stop!"

Eric's command was ignored. Farrell ran at her again, full speed. Hailey knew if she was going to bring him in, now was the time to do it. There would be no satisfaction in killing the man.

She grabbed the nearest folding chair, hefted the thing up and swung it at Farrell, hitting him in the side of the head. The pain in her hand was blinding.

Farrell flew back with the force of it and landed in the aisle. Eric holstered his weapon, grabbed Farrell's arms and subdued him.

Hailey turned back to Kerry. "I told you to run."

She grabbed Kerry's hand and they went together to the main door through which Hailey had entered. Her gun was nowhere to be seen. But Farrell wasn't going anywhere for a while, not if Eric had anything to do with it.

She ushered Kerry along in front of her. They had to get to Charles in the boat and get out of there. "You were supposed to be with Jonah."

"Farrell shot him." Kerry whimpered. "There was so much blood."

Images of Jonah bleeding in dirty river water flooded Hailey's mind. "What happened?"

"We were in Jonah's car. All the way from the warehouse up to Frank's bluff was still above the water."

Hailey nodded. It would be, though possibly not for much longer, which was likely why the county sheriff had ordered total evacuation.

Kerry sniffed. "We were stopped by a downed tree and Jonah got out to see if there was any way around it. Farrell came out of nowhere. He shot Jonah and got in the car."

Just like when he'd tried to abduct her, Farrell hadn't attempted to kill Kerry. He'd needed her in his grasp... for leverage against Hailey. No parent should have to face that reality for their child. The thought stirred rage and disgust in her toward Farrell—even more than she'd felt for him before.

Eric grappled with Farrell, trying to hold him still with nothing to restrain him.

"We're going to the boat. Maybe there's rope."

Eric looked up. "No, wait for—"

Hailey crossed the foyer and flung the main doors open.

Marshal Turner stood on the front step, his face twisted with rage. His gun was pointed straight at Hailey and Kerry. Beyond Turner, Charles was slumped over in the boat.

Please, don't be dead. Kerry needs you even if you do go to jail.

Hailey tucked her daughter behind her back. "Couldn't wait for your retirement check?"

Turner snorted. "I always liked you, Shelder. But it's never worth waiting for something that might not even be there. Not when you can take the payout now."

Hailey figured what Turner had said was probably the motto of dirty cops everywhere. She might even be inclined to feel sorry for him, if she wasn't so certain the bullet he shot would go straight through her into Kerry.

Turner looked beyond her, into the church, and hollered, "Farrell!"

TWENTY-FOUR

Hailey turned Kerry aside, giving Turner line of sight to where Eric held Farrell. The escapee was moaning and trying to get up. Water splashed under her boots. She looked down. It was two inches deep and rising.

This whole night was going from bad to worse with no end in sight. Jonah was likely dead. Eric was holding Farrell, which meant it was up to Hailey to get them out of this. Behind her, Hailey heard Kerry quietly pray for help and safety. Her daughter's wisdom was like the sun bursting through these dark clouds.

Jesus, we need You.

Hailey walked backward, taking Kerry with her. She looked at Turner, who was aiming his gun at her. "How long have you been working with Farrell?"

The marshal shrugged. "Does it matter?"

On the off-chance he got caught, he likely didn't want to implicate himself. But Turner had killed already today, so he was probably planning to get rid of all of them and simply walk away with his freedom and the jewels. It would take days for police to unravel the mess after the river washed all the evidence away.

Hailey's life might not have been perfect…or even particularly happy, but she didn't want to go out that way. And she certainly wasn't going to let the same thing happen to Kerry or Eric.

Turner kept his gun trained on them. "Now, where are the jewels?"

Eric's jaw was clenched. She could see it even from this distance. He shifted as Farrell struggled in his grip.

Farrell's eyes flickered. He knew now that the bag she'd given him didn't contain the actual jewels, and yet he wasn't telling Turner. Had Farrell been planning to double-cross Turner this whole time?

Hailey moved to the side so she and Kerry weren't between the two men facing off against each other.

Someone grunted, and Eric yelled. Hailey turned just as the sound was cut off by a dull thud. Farrell grabbed for a dazed Eric's gun. *Farrell had hit him?* They wrestled, and the gun went off. Farrell backed up, Eric's weapon in his hand.

Eric slumped to the floor, blood streaming from his temple.

Farrell stood with the bag in one hand and Eric's gun in the other. "Ready to go. After I deal this one some retribution." He motioned to Hailey.

Turner shook his head. "We don't have time for your fun and games."

Hailey figured he'd already done her enough damage. But without her weapon, and against two armed men, there wasn't much she could do. She moved farther back, bringing Kerry with her and praying with everything she had that neither man would notice the widening gap between them and the girls in the church foyer.

Farrell's eyes flashed. "I didn't say it would take long."

Eric didn't stir.

Turner stood his ground just inside the church doors.

"Just kill them, and I'll get you out of town. Everyone who knows what you did will be dead."

It figured Turner would want Farrell to kill them. But would he? Did Farrell know the marshal was just getting Farrell to implicate himself further? Turner would probably kill Farrell the first chance he got, take the jewels and hide them and claim he brought Eric, Hailey and Kerry's killer to justice.

He would walk away free.

Farrell's lips thinned. "You mean everyone will be dead except you."

He whipped his gun hand toward Turner and fired. Turner dropped to the floor, letting off shot after shot in Farrell's direction as he fell. Hailey dived, covering Kerry with her body. Something slammed into her vest. It was like being hit point-blank with a shot from a paintball gun. Or one of those bean-bag rounds she'd been hit with at the airport.

Kerry screamed. Hailey tried to get her breath back, but her side hurt as much as her hand now.

She wasn't going to survive this.

"Eric!"

He shifted, his eyes glassy. Did he even know what was going on? He glanced around.

Farrell was going to kill them all. But she was going to make sure Kerry got out if it was the last thing she did. Hailey shifted off Kerry.

The back door was across the sanctuary. "Go. Now. Out the back way." Hailey used her best don't-argue-with-me voice. Kerry whimpered, but clambered to her feet and made a run for it.

Hailey stood and faced Farrell's weapon. Pain screamed from her hand and her side. She lifted her chin even though she still didn't have a gun. "You really are under arrest."

He laughed.

Still on the floor, Eric's attention was on Farrell, and it looked like he was trying to focus. The escapee lifted his gun at the same time her partner swung his leg up and slammed it into the back of Farrell's knees. Farrell started to fall.

The gun went flying.

Hailey slammed into him and they rolled over and over, until Hailey's head hit a chair.

Hailey's face was in the water. Eric hauled her out just as he'd done with Kerry and saw Turner beyond her, dead from a gunshot to his chest.

"Where did Farrell go?" Hailey shook off her daze.

"He made a run for it." Eric pulled Hailey with him to the door where Kerry was.

He pulled both of them into his arms and held them tight. Hailey took sharp breaths, like she was fighting tears, while Kerry had already yielded to hers.

Hailey pulled back. "Thank you."

Eric held her gaze. "I should have been in there quicker. I can't believe he got the drop on me."

"It's okay. It's done now."

She was right. They were safe. "Let's get to Charles."

"I think Turner did something to him."

Eric saw her face and didn't ask more questions she wouldn't want to answer in front of Charles's daughter.

Turner's actions had vindicated Eric, proving his statement about Turner's earlier murder of Mr. Phelps, but that wasn't going to help them any right now.

Hailey led them back through the church to the front door. Turner was still lying where he'd fallen. They skirted the edge of the room, and Eric kept himself between Kerry and the dead man. He didn't want her to have to see that.

Hailey went for the door and he pulled her back. "Let me. Stay here with Kerry, out of the rain."

Hailey nodded. Still, he could see in her eyes that she understood his real reason for wanting them to stay there. Charles was Kerry's father, and if he was dead then she didn't need that image on top of everything else she'd seen that night.

Eric waded to where Jonah's boat had drifted against the building. Charles was alive, slumped inside, and the other boat—Turner's—was still tethered to the other railing of the front steps, opposite where they'd tied Jonah's boat. Farrell could be gone as easily as he could still be in the building. What kind of boat did he have?

Eric waved Kerry and Hailey outside and got them loaded into Turner's boat. He held Hailey's elbow, helping her onto the boat. She hissed and touched a hand to her side.

"Okay?"

"Vest. Probably just a bruise." Or she had a cracked rib from the impact of the gunshot. Eric didn't think either was likely to slow her down, given the fact she was running on pure adrenaline. This needed to end. Now.

Charles was heavier than he looked, but Eric hauled him to the boat and set him beside Kerry. He had a huge knot on his forehead. Eric faced the fact he needed to take care of them. He needed to get Hailey, Kerry and Charles to safety before he continued the search for Farrell.

Hailey might even need serious medical attention, and there was no telling how bad Charles's injury was. Head wounds were tricky. Eric should know, since there was blood running down his own face. It wasn't a bad cut, but it was bleeding steadily.

Kerry brushed back her father's hair. She looked happy

to have something to focus on other than the mess they were in. She probably got that from her mother.

Hailey scanned the area.

Eric fired up the boat and they pulled away. Farrell darted out of the building, but mid-turn, Eric didn't have the angle right to head back to the fugitive. They were facing the wrong way. Hailey shouted, "Down!"

Kerry didn't hesitate. She dived beside her father and nearly hit her head on the bench. Was that how Charles got the knot on his head, cowering from Turner? Kerry covered her head with her hands.

Farrell lifted his gun, aiming at their boat. Eric let Hailey take the motor and aimed his weapon at Farrell. The two men faced off while Eric's boat drifted downstream and Farrell fired up Jonah's boat engine to tear off in the opposite direction.

"We have to get him," Hailey yelled.

"We will. But it's not worth all our lives."

"Drop us off and then go."

Eric looked at her, shocked she would suggest that. "You want me to go alone?"

"I need to be with Kerry, but you should get Farrell. Take us back to the church. Drop us off and get Farrell, Eric."

He pressed his lips together. Hailey was already turning the boat around, heading back to the church. Farrell was far away already. Eric couldn't even see him anymore.

An alarm blared loud enough it could be heard from one end of town to the other.

The dam was failing.

"We have to get in the church. We'll get washed away otherwise." Eric looked back at where Farrell had gone. "He's got a good head start."

"You're going to let that stop you?"

Eric narrowed his eyes and looked at her. "Don't bait me into rushing off without thinking this through. I'm not going to respond to a challenge. I'm going to do my job. But first you all need to be safe."

Kerry gasped. "The boat isn't safe?"

Eric shook his head. "When the wall of water comes, the boat will be washed away. I need to get to Farrell before that happens."

They bumped the stairs and Hailey helped Kerry out of the boat. She shot him a look. "You can't let him get away."

"I won't. You know that." Eric hefted Charles into the foyer and set him down. If the water washed the boat away, it would likely be smashed to pieces against a building. Then how would they get to safety?

"Be careful."

"First you tell me to go get Farrell, and now you're telling me to be careful?"

Hailey rolled her eyes. She grabbed the collar of his jacket and pulled him toward her. When their faces were an inch apart, she said, "If you get hurt I'm going to be really mad at you."

Eric laughed. "Likewise. Be safe, okay?"

Hailey pulled him the rest of the way in and planted a kiss on his lips. Not one to be outdone, Eric caught her up in his arms and lifted her off her feet as he deepened the kiss to the point Kerry said, "That's just gross."

Eric pulled back, sharing a smile with Hailey. "I'll be back soon."

"Sure, we'll be fine."

He headed outside, where the wall of water was a gigantic swell.

And it was headed right for them.

TWENTY-FIVE

Eric ducked back inside and shut the door. Charles shifted on the floor and groaned. Eric lifted him up by his armpits. "Wake up, Mr. Mayor. It's time to go."

Hailey's eyes widened. "What is it?"

"Water is coming, faster than I thought. Are there stairs anywhere that'll take us up to the roof?"

Kerry squeaked. "The roof?"

He dragged Charles and ran after Hailey, who hauled Kerry by her arm to a side door. They climbed stairs into a loft room full of folding tables and chairs, with boxes piled high. The building shook beneath them, like something heavy had slammed into the side of it.

Charles moaned. "What's going on?"

"You've gotta wake up, dude." The guy had put Kerry and Hailey in danger. Eric would rather leave him in the church to drown, but that wasn't the kind of man he was.

Hailey pulled down a ladder, straightening it and clicking it into place by jumping on the bottom rung. She pulled Kerry up first and followed her through the hatch.

Charles blinked and looked at Eric with blurry eyes.

"Your turn."

Charles labored slowly up the ladder. Eric followed mostly to make sure he didn't fall. Water rushed over the

opening in the roof and poured on them. Charles yelped
and let go of the ladder. Eric grabbed him and bodily
forced Charles to keep climbing.

Charles made it to the roof, where he collapsed on the
wet tiles. Eric shifted the man's legs out of the way and
climbed out of the hatch. Hailey grabbed his hand and
helped him stand. All of them looked around. The roof
was like the tall island in the middle of a lake. The tops
of the houses barely peeked out of the water, lined up in
rows like crackers in soup.

"Farrell!"

Kerry's yell jerked them all around. Charles sat up, rub-
bing the knot on his head. Eric looked past her pointed finger to where Farrell was climbing out of the water at least
a quarter mile away. His flashlight bobbed as he surveyed
the area, probably looking for a way out of this mess. Farrell turned and saw them. He immediately reached around
his waistband, but came up empty.

"He's unarmed." Hailey's statement seemed to echo
in the air.

Eric turned back to Kerry. "Stay here with your dad,
okay? Don't go anywhere."

Kerry nodded.

Eric looked at Hailey. "I'm going."

His partner unzipped her jacket and ripped off her bulletproof vest. "I'm coming, too."

Hailey swam behind Eric to the nearest roof. Her side
hurt, but she was ninety percent sure her ribs were just
bruised. Water weighed down her clothes, despite the fact
she'd removed her jacket and shoes, but she put one hand
in front of the other over and over again.

They needed Farrell alive if he was going to own up
to everything he'd put them through over the weekend. It

wasn't enough for Farrell to be stopped—Hailey wanted justice for what he'd done. Part of her wanted the same from Charles. Justice for his selfish actions. For Kerry's sake she could forgive his stupidity, so long as he treated his daughter like the precious gem she was for the rest of her life. Whether he was in prison or not.

Eric pulled himself up onto the first roof like he was barely winded. He reached down, and Hailey clasped his hand with her good one. He pulled her up, and she sucked in breaths. She ran distance for her workouts, but apparently swimming used a whole different set of muscles.

"No rain for six months when this is done. I don't think that's too much to ask for, do you?" She looked up, but Eric wasn't smiling. He was staring off into the distance.

Farrell was gone.

Hailey shifted, looking around. "Where is he?"

Eric strode over the peak of the roof to the other side. "I didn't see him go and I don't see him ahead of us."

"So he's in the water?"

"Let's get over there and find out."

Eric backed up two steps and made a run for it, leaping to the next roof. Hailey did the same. The feeling of weightlessness brought a split second of panic before she hit the next roof. *Thank the good Lord for row houses.*

She straightened, and Eric caught the look on her face. "What?"

Hailey backed up for the next jump. "I always hated these houses. Now I'm kind of glad they're cookie-cutter, all packed together."

They jumped between three more roofs before they neared the one where Farrell had been. Jonah's boat was nowhere in sight.

Two more jumps followed, and then they were on the roof where he'd been standing before. The flashlight Farrell had been holding now lay in the gutter, lighting up the surface of the water.

Murky liquid surrounded them on all sides. Hailey looked back to where Kerry stood. With one hand above her eyes to shield her face from the rain, Kerry peered at them. Charles was slumped on the roof beside her.

Farrell was still nowhere in sight.

Hailey reached down to grab the flashlight.

Fingers broke the surface of the water, wrapped around her forearm and pulled her in. Hailey fell face-first into murky water that rushed up her nose and down her throat. Someone wrapped around her, holding her immobile as she sank down in the cold water between two houses.

She struggled to surface. Her lungs burned fire through her throat, but she couldn't move against his grip. She just sank farther and farther down.

Someone collided with them, knocking Farrell against her. The world was a dark ocean, and Hailey didn't know which way was up and which way was down.

Farrell jerked like he was being pulled away from her. She struggled harder, praying Eric would get him away from her so she could get to the surface and breathe.

Farrell's grip on her was like an iron vice.

Spots peppered the edges of her vision. Hailey knew it was only a short amount of time before she surrendered to the urge to breathe and gulped in a lungful of water that would kill her.

She was jerked back and forth until Farrell let go with one arm. Hailey could barely see. She fought more and more, trying to get loose, but Farrell's legs bound her. She could feel them both sink farther down.

Sooner or later they would hit the bottom.

Farrell fell away from her like dead weight. Hailey was free. She tried to move her arms and legs, but they wouldn't respond to her brain's signals despite the force of her will to live. To get to the surface so she could breathe.

Kerry.

Eric.

Hailey wanted to hug her dad and tell him she was sorry for being such an awful daughter. She'd been in so much pain over everyone's opinion of her, and neither of them had known how to fix it. But that was no excuse for being such a jerk to him.

It was too late.

Eric surfaced, sucking in breaths as the world brightened. Dragged under again, he kicked until his head broke out of the water. Even as unconscious, dead weight Farrell was still intent on hauling him back down to his death.

Eric lifted Farrell's head out of the water and glanced around.

He'd almost lost his mind when Hailey was submerged. Farrell's grip was unrelenting, but Eric had finally hit the man hard enough Farrell was forced to let his partner go.

When he could tread water no longer, Eric hauled Farrell onto the roof and looked around.

Why hadn't Hailey surfaced?

He waited, certain she would break the water any second looking as bedraggled as he felt. Any second.

Come on, Hailey.

Eric grabbed the flashlight from where it lay in the gutter. He took three deep breaths and dived down. The light barely penetrated the dense blackness as he swept his arm back and forth. He searched down to the bottom, where the drenched earth gave against his weight, but still couldn't see her.

God, where is she?

His lungs demanded air. Eric raced to the surface,

sucked in another breath and forced himself back down, moving his search farther away. Had she drifted this distance?

He kept searching the dark waters, not willing to lose her to the river. He wouldn't let Kerry grow up motherless. *You don't want her to die either.*

That was true. Not because she was a focused and driven partner. She was more important than that, more important *to him* than that.

Eric pushed through the water and finally found her, pale-faced, floating just above the ground. Her lips were blue and her hair hung around her head like a red halo.

Was she dead?

TWENTY-SIX

It didn't matter if he'd never found her—Eric would have kept searching the river for eternity.

Emotion rushed through him, making his head swim with more than lack of oxygen. He grabbed her and made for the surface, knowing for sure now that he loved this woman. More than anyone he'd ever known.

His head cleared the water, and he gasped for air. He hauled them both onto the roof and laid Hailey down. He checked her pulse, but there wasn't one. She wasn't breathing.

Eric tilted her head and began CPR.

Hands yanked him away from her. Eric spun around and saw Farrell a split second before the punch slammed into his jaw. Bright light splintered behind Eric's eyes. He stumbled, recovered and hit Farrell back. Eric's nose started to bleed again.

Farrell punched at him, a vicious combination that dazed Eric. Wet clothes weighed down his arms and legs. Farrell's arm closed around Eric's neck and pulled him into a headlock. All he could see was Hailey, as good as dead on the roof with little to no chance of coming back from it.

God, I have to get to her. She can't die. She can't.

In the distance he could hear Kerry screaming and Charles yelling.

He struggled against Farrell's grip, reached up from the headlock he was in and grabbed the sides of Farrell's face. He pulled with every ounce of strength he had left and managed to flip Farrell over.

Farrell slammed his head on the roof. With him dazed, and hopefully unconscious, Eric ran to Hailey.

Eric got through two rounds of chest compressions and breaths before a booted foot slammed into his side, knocking him over. He straightened, ignoring his assailant, and started up again, pumping Hailey's chest and willing her to breathe. Farrell kicked him in the side of the head.

Kerry cried out, the sound ringing in Eric's ears. He couldn't let her down. Eric ignored the throbbing in his body and leaned down to breathe life back into Hailey.

Farrell reared back and kicked him again in the side.

He breathed.

Farrell kicked.

Hailey jerked and began to sputter. Eric flipped her onto her side, where she coughed river water onto the roof. Farrell kicked him again, bursting fire in Eric's ribs. He grabbed the escapee's foot, twisted it and planted Farrell prone on the roof.

He listened to the blessed sound of Hailey's sputtering while he punched and kicked the man who nearly killed her.

At the first opening, Eric flipped Farrell facedown and grasped the man's hands behind his back. "Enough!"

Eric dumped Farrell at the far end of the roof, where he sat muttering something under his breath that Hailey was pretty sure was not complimentary to either her or Eric.

Eric turned back to where she was sitting. The look on

his face was like he hadn't seen her in a decade. Hailey didn't know what to make of it, especially when he sat with her and drew her into his arms. She rested against his shoulder and listened to the rise and fall of his chest while her head swam. His breath hitched.

"What is it?"

Eric looked out at the water. "Farrell kicked me in the ribs. I think he cracked one with his boot."

Hailey shot a glare at Farrell. As if the man hadn't done enough damage to them. Thankfully, all they had to do now was bring the escapee back in and get him booked into custody. Then he would be out of state, finally serving his federal time in California, and they could get on with their lives.

Hailey's head throbbed. Had she hit it on something? She didn't much care, snuggled into Eric's side. What had happened?

When Farrell was gone, Eric would go back to being her partner and Hailey would…what? She wasn't sure who she would be. Not after this weekend.

"You okay?"

Hailey looked up at him. His face was inches from hers, and he didn't look much better than she felt. But instead of seeing relief in his face, all she saw was unease. "Are *you* okay?"

"Don't ever do that to me again."

"Fall in the river?" She nearly laughed.

"No. Stop breathing."

Hailey's body went solid. "I…I wasn't breathing?"

Eric nodded. "I gave you mouth-to-mouth."

"But you said Farrell kicked you…"

"I know."

"I don't understand." Hailey stared at him while she processed what he was saying.

No wonder her brain felt like it wasn't running at full capacity. Her muscles felt like water. Farrell could swim away to escape forever and she'd probably just sit there and not care. It would take too much energy to go after him. She was completely spent.

Hailey lifted one hand, the extent of her physical capabilities, and rested it against Eric's jaw. "Thank you."

He held her gaze with his. "You're welcome."

"Thank you."

"I said you're welcome."

Hailey nodded as much as she could, which was still only a slight movement. "I know. Thank you. For me, for Kerry. For my dad. For all of us. Really. Seriously. Thank you."

She didn't realize she was crying until she felt the wetness on her cheeks. Eric swiped away the tears with his thumbs, leaned down and covered her lips with his. Lips that had breathed life back into her.

Hailey's breath hitched. She buried her face in his shoulder and held tight until the emotion subsided. Then she lifted her head and looked to where Charles and Kerry were sitting together on the roof of the church.

There was no way to get to them, not without swimming while hauling Farrell with them. There was no way Hailey could make it that far without Eric's help, and he couldn't do that and keep Farrell contained at the same time.

Her eyes locked with her daughter's and Hailey raised her hand, palm facing out. Kerry shifted in the shelter of her dad's arms and did the same. Hailey gave her a smile. However furious she was for what Charles had done and the danger he'd put them in, he was still taking care of Kerry, and the girl would always love her father. That was just the kind of person her daughter was.

Eric's hand rubbed up and down Hailey's back and she

huddled into his warmth. She tore her gaze from Kerry. "What are we going to do now?"

Eric drew out his phone. "No signal. Jonah knew where we were—"

"Jonah's probably dead."

Eric's arms tightened around her, as though he needed strength as badly as she did. "So no one knows where we are?"

Hailey pressed her lips together. "Someone will find us. They have to."

"But how long will that take? We can't last out here forever, soaking wet and exhausted."

A smirk curled Farrell's lips. Hailey lifted her chin and glared at him. It was a feeble attempt to show him that despite everything he'd done, she might be down but she wasn't broken. Still, it made her feel better.

She turned back to Eric. "Don't give up now. We need you to keep faith until the end. I need you to."

He studied her face but didn't say anything.

"You can't quit now." She pointed at Farrell, though neither of them looked that way. "We got our man. We're safe. Kerry is safe. Everything will turn out fine. We just have to trust God, since He's brought us this far."

Eric's face softened. "You're right. He brought me to you."

Hailey grasped Eric's cheeks in her hands and pulled his face down so that his lips touched her forehead. Her heart swelled with love, but she couldn't tell him that. Not when it had happened so fast. Just days before this they had only been partners, and not even full partners who relied on and trusted each other. Now they were so much more.

Hailey would fight for this. She couldn't let things go back to the way they had been before. Acquaintances. Coworkers. She wouldn't be able to bear it if that happened.

It would hurt worse than never having found out what could be between them, if she let him go knowing what she had lost.

Hailey tried to hold her grip on his face. "Don't let go."

"I won't."

"Not ever."

"I promise I won't let go, Hailey."

Her breath hitched. Eric's lips touched her forehead, and she squeezed her eyes shut, hardly caring that the escapee was seeing them like this.

Eric's head moved and his lips rested by her ear. "I—"

A helicopter crested the mountain behind them. Hailey turned to see it fly toward them, her heart aching to hear what Eric might have been about to say. Could he really feel the same way she did? Wouldn't that have been crazy? They'd only known each other a few days.

Eric wrapped her up more tightly. Hailey started to ask what was going on when the spray of water hit her. The helicopter steadied itself overhead.

The whomp of the rotors was deafening, making Hailey's head swim. She was going to have to go up in that thing? It was going to weave around, dip and tilt, and she would have to hang on.

She moved her mouth so she could speak directly in Eric's ear. "Is it the National Guard?"

Eric nodded. "And they brought a friend."

The tone in his voice brought her head up. Hailey looked through the spray at the man now strapping himself into a harness. He wasn't wearing the fatigues the others in the helicopter had on. His jeans were getting soaked and the hood on his rain jacket had flown back. This man's hair was a different shade of blond from Eric's, but she could make out his features as he descended to the roof.

Hailey looked at Eric. "That's your brother."

He flexed his jaw. "Yep. That's Aaron, all right."

It wasn't the first time Hailey had seen and heard the tension in him when he spoke of his brother. She'd always wondered what it would be like to have a sibling. Now that she was seeing it in action, she realized it was a lot like her relationship with her dad.

When they saw each other day in and day out, Hailey let her frustration get the best of her and took it out on him, knowing he would always love her. Then when he was gone she missed him—like now, when she desperately wanted to find out if he was all right and give him a hug.

She was a horrible daughter.

Eric glanced at her and frowned. "What's wrong?"

"I need to find my dad."

He gave her a squeeze. "We'll find him as soon as we can, okay? He should be at the Falcons' stadium with everyone else."

Hailey nodded. One by one they were loaded into the helicopter. Aaron looked at her with a fair amount of curiosity. He glanced between her and Eric, and his curiosity seemed to pique when Eric explained that she was his partner. But then he grinned with Eric's smile and Hailey found she could relax a little.

She ignored Farrell, who was being handcuffed to the bar on the ceiling of the helicopter, and gripped the seat belt strapping her in. Eric pulled her hand between both of his as they flew the short distance to where Kerry and Charles were. When Aaron moved to strap in and descend for them, Eric stopped him with a hand.

"Let me. I want to be the one to get her."

TWENTY-SEVEN

The helicopter landed in the parking lot at the Falcons' stadium. The place was lit up and swarming with people.

"Grandpa's in there somewhere."

Hailey turned to Kerry and yelled back, "We'll find him."

"But we don't know for sure that he made it here. He could be at home, or stuck somewhere." Kerry's voice was thin.

Hailey shifted Kerry's face into her shoulder. She could try to convince her daughter everything would work out. After all, Kerry only had to look around the helicopter to see what they'd overcome together, to see how God had brought them all through the flood. But her strength had faded and at this point she doubted she could walk, let alone come up with a helpful answer.

Still, Hailey knew nothing soothed a person better than touch. That's why she didn't mind being squished up against Eric in the chopper. Or the fact that he'd reached for her hand when he'd settled beside her with Kerry, and he hadn't let go.

He would let go eventually, but she wasn't going to think about that.

Once police officers secured Farrell and escorted

Charles away, Eric climbed out of the helicopter. Hailey sent Kerry in front of her so Eric could help her out. His attention to Kerry warmed her, as did the way he reached again for her hand.

Hailey scooted to the edge, but energy bled from her muscles until she suddenly had no strength left.

When she stopped, Aaron stepped forward. "You okay?"

She couldn't even lift her head.

Eric came over, still holding Kerry's hand. "What's wrong?"

"I don't know," Aaron said. "She just stopped."

"Hailey?"

She tried to focus on his voice. The world tilted and hands steadied her. Eric's voice floated in and out of her consciousness. She heard only the words "drowned" and "CPR."

A man's arms surrounded her shoulders, hooked under her knees and lifted her. Hailey's world vacillated between darkness and bright floodlights. People talked, their voices going in and out.

When she blinked again, the ceiling was miles away. Hailey tried to sit up, but Aaron put his hand on her shoulder. "Easy."

The world spun. "Where's Kerry?"

"Eric took her to get hot chocolate and some breakfast."

"Breakfast?"

Aaron gave her a sympathetic smile. "It's morning. You've been out for hours."

Hailey's stomach unclenched. "Did Eric get his ribs looked at?"

A gleam of something flashed in Aaron's eyes. "Care about my brother, do you?"

"Of course." Hailey didn't like the suspicion on his face.

She'd spent years trying to prove herself to everyone but no more. She was who God had made her to be, and that was all she could be. "He's my partner. Why wouldn't I care that he got treatment?"

"Are you sure that's all he is?"

Hailey shifted on the bed. She was surrounded by rows of other beds in what looked like a back room of the stadium. She didn't want to be evasive, but this was Eric's brother. And she hadn't even told Eric how she felt yet.

"Eric and I work together. We care about each other." She paused. "Now if you'll excuse me, I need to rest, not get the third degree from you."

"I'll let Eric and Kerry know you're awake."

"See if you can find anything out about Jonah Rivers while you're there."

Aaron glanced back and grinned. "Yes, ma'am."

Hailey bunched up her pillows and managed to sit up. Kerry had seen her pass out, but she didn't need to come back and see Hailey looking sick, no matter how bad she felt.

"Hailey?"

Her head whipped around to the source of that voice. Her dad shuffled over, his coat wrapped tight around his body by his folded arms. He grabbed her hand and pulled it to his chest.

"Dad, you're okay." Hailey shifted over and he settled on the bed. "You are, aren't you? Charles said you have cancer."

His face shut down, and it was then that Hailey knew.

"Why didn't you tell me?"

"I just…I tried. I had every intention of telling you, but I'd open my mouth and…I just couldn't." He breathed, slow and quiet. "All I could think of was your face when your mom and I told you that your mom had it. That whole time she was sick, and then after she died, it was like you died, too. I mean, you were still walking around, but part of you was gone. So I started treatment and—"

Hailey's heart swelled with love for her dad. He'd been trying to protect her from the pain she'd experienced watching her mom die. She realized something. "When you had the flu?"

Her dad's eyes lifted, full of guilt and pain. "That's what I told you."

"And I believed you." She wanted to yell at him, but only because she felt a truckload of guilt herself for being so wrapped up in her own life that she took his word for it. Instead of digging a little and realizing something much bigger was going on.

But that was before. Things were going to be a whole lot different now, starting with her relationship with her dad.

"I'm so sorry." She pulled him close and kissed his cheek. "I should have been a better daughter. I should've realized."

He kissed her back. "And I should have told you."

"Do you need anything?" Hailey glanced around, wondering if there was anyone nearby who knew anything about her dad's condition. "Do you need any help right now? We could get you a bed."

He shook his head. "I'm good now, darlin'. Finished my treatment and got a clean bill of health."

"Really?"

He grunted, which at any other time would have been a laugh. "Sure did, for now at least. I just have to keep an eye on things and get regular checkups. But my insides are clear."

Hailey smiled. One day she'd get him to actually say out loud the precise location of the cancer. But more likely he'd just leave some paperwork out, and she'd read it there instead. Because why wouldn't they communicate that way, when the alternative was him saying something he thought was "delicate" out loud?

Hailey sighed. "I'm glad you're okay, Dad."

"Me, too, darlin'. Me, too." He grinned. "Now tell me about this partner of yours. You tell him you like him yet?"

Hailey tried to laugh but choked instead. "Uh, not yet, exactly."

"Well, why ever not?"

Hailey shook her head. "Maybe because I haven't seen him since I came to?"

"That wouldn't have stopped me. When I realized it wasn't food poisoning and that I loved your mother, I didn't let anything stop me. Not my carburetor, or her dad and his shotgun. I left my car at home and rode my bike across town to the ranch and got down on one knee in front of the stables."

Hailey couldn't believe it. "You never told me that! You guys were sweethearts?"

His grizzled face nodded. "Never met anyone like her, and never have since."

"Did she say yes?"

"Yeah, but only when she stopped laughing. Then I kissed her and she didn't mind that I was all sweaty. She told me she loved me. It was like finally everything clicked into place and I knew where I was supposed to be. Who I was supposed to be."

"Charles and I were sweethearts, once. Why did you hate it so much when I got pregnant?"

Her dad's face darkened. "That girl of yours is sweet as anything, but Charles was never the man for you."

"You knew that?"

His lips twitched. "Fathers always know."

Hailey gave him a small smile. She wasn't even going

to comment on that one. "My life got so messed up, but Kerry makes it right in so many ways. More than I ever believed she would. But can I really expect a guy to want an instant family? We come with our fair share of drama, and maybe he can't handle that. What if he doesn't want to try?"

Hailey's dad touched her cheeks with his rough hands and kissed her forehead. "If he doesn't, then he's a big idiot."

Hailey laughed.

"Seriously, he doesn't deserve you if he doesn't want both you and Kerry."

"Thanks, Dad." She still wasn't convinced she was actually going to tell Eric how she felt. It would mess up too much of their lives if he didn't feel the same way she did. Sure, he'd given her mouth-to-mouth. And he had seemed like he really didn't want to lose her.

But that didn't mean he thought of her as anything more than a friend and partner.

TWENTY-EIGHT

Eric waited with Aaron so that Kerry could talk to Hailey before he did. Really, he didn't know what he was going to say when he saw her. After the weekend they'd had, he was liable to gush all over her out of sheer relief that she wasn't dead, which was probably the last thing Hailey needed.

Later, when Eric could control his emotions, he would sit down with her and they could find their feet as partners. Things wouldn't go back to the way they'd been three days ago. They had a new equilibrium because of what they'd been through, and things would be better now. They would be stronger and closer partners, and Eric was fine with it. Why did he need to risk messing that up?

He didn't need it to be more. That was a selfish desire he couldn't put on Hailey. She didn't need to bear the burden of his shortcomings just because he was now so much more aware of what was missing in his life.

Aaron nudged Eric's arm. Eric looked over and realized his brother had been watching him watch Kerry and Hailey. "Really?"

Eric frowned. "What?" Aaron always thought he knew everything about everything when he didn't. "Why did you come here, anyway?"

Aaron's eyebrows rose. "Maybe because you were stuck

on a roof and needed rescuing? I know it burns you to even consider that you might still need me to help you, and I'm sorry you feel that way. I guess I thought I was being a good brother every time I looked out for you. Maybe I did it wrong—"

Eric cut in. "That isn't it." He sighed. "I wanted to stand up for myself. I didn't want…"

"What?"

"To need you."

Aaron's face softened, his expression dangerously too close to pity for Eric's liking. "It's not bad to need someone, Eric. That's what family is supposed to be." He paused. "I had to learn it, too. To let go of my need to be self-sufficient and trust God, but also to give some of that trust to Mackenzie. Not because my wife had earned it, but because I wanted to share it with her."

Right. Like it was that easy to just give up what he'd fought to hold on to for years. Eric shook his head. Hailey didn't need that from him. She had her life, her dad and her daughter. That was a full plate without him adding to it.

But God? That was a whole other question.

In the heat of the moment, when Hailey hadn't been breathing and Farrell was attacking him, Eric had asked God for help. Aaron looked to God for everything. Could Eric do the same, or would that mean he'd lose part of himself in the process?

"One last thing and then I'll get out of your hair…forever if you need it." Aaron squeezed his shoulder. "When you give your trust away to God, and to someone who will treasure it, that doesn't mean you lose something. Believe me when I tell you, you gain more than you could ever imagine. But you have to take that step of faith.

"I know you want your life to be more than it is right now, because I felt the same way. I was scared to jump off the ledge and trust that Mackenzie could believe in me the way I believe in her."

Eric gave his brother a look. "I thought the idea was to quit trying to save me."

"You know me." Aaron grinned. "I can't help it." Then his smile dropped and he said, "Seriously, though, God gave you to me as a brother, and I don't ever want to take that for granted."

Eric worked his jaw back and forth and finally managed to say, "I love you, you know."

Aaron squeezed the tendons between Eric's neck and shoulder. "I know." He grinned and motioned to where Hailey was sitting, holding Kerry. "Now go make sure *she* knows it."

Hailey held Kerry. Her daughter was in her arms, but in front of her like a shield, and Hailey realized she'd been doing that for years. She'd kept herself at arm's length from everyone and everything that might demand something of her.

Could she really be more than a mother and a marshal? Could she be a wife, too?

Eric skirted between beds and people, making his way to where she and Kerry were sitting.

He looked exhausted, like he needed three days' worth of sleep to get back to normal. But when he stood next to the bed, he smiled. "Feel better?"

Hailey squeezed Kerry. "I do now."

Kerry shifted on her lap, glancing between Hailey and Eric. "Are you guys boyfriend and girlfriend now?"

Hailey froze. She didn't dare look at Eric in case he thought it was a horrible idea.

He settled on the edge of the bed. "How would you feel about that, Kerry?"

Kerry held herself completely still. "If you got married, would you be my stepdad?"

Hailey looked up. Eric's face was frozen like he hadn't even thought of that. He cleared his throat. "It's up to your mom, but if it's okay with you...I'd like that."

Hailey squeezed Kerry and motioned to where her friends were waiting. "Why don't you go talk to Janessa and Valerie, okay? I need to talk to Eric for a minute."

Kerry hopped off the bed.

Hailey waited until she was out of earshot and then turned to Eric. "You didn't have to say that. You're too nice, but you can't tell a child that you'll be their parent if you don't mean it. It isn't fair to Kerry for you to make that promise. You have to tell her. You have to take it back—"

Eric covered her mouth with his hand. "What if I did mean it?" Hailey shifted on the bed. His hand dropped and he took her hands in his. "Hailey?"

She looked up and saw all the love and fear and nerves she felt, there in his eyes. Then his lips curled up into a grin. "So what do you say? Are we boyfriend and girlfriend now?"

She wanted to laugh, but instead she cleared her throat. "If we do this, there's no taking it back. It will change everything."

"For the better, I hope."

"What if we wreck it?"

He squeezed her hands. "How about this? What do you say we go out to dinner or a movie or something, with Kerry? We can do it again by ourselves. Will you give me a chance to prove to you how good this can be?"

"Aren't you scared?"

"Honestly?" He scratched the side of his head, a move that made him look years younger. "Yes, I am. But I'm trying to trust God. I don't think He would have brought me here and given me you if He hadn't planned something better than I already had. Maybe I had to lose my job with WITSEC so that I could be with you."

"Because I needed you."

His eyebrows lifted. "Do you, really?"

"Don't tell anyone." Hailey smiled. "I think dating sounds like a great idea."

"To start with."

"What?"

He shrugged. "I've never seen the point in dating if it's not leading to…more."

Hailey blinked. He wanted to marry her? She loved him, but wasn't it too soon to be having that conversation?

"So we'll call it courting."

Hailey leaned closer and whispered, "I don't know how to do that." What if she messed it up?

"The only thing you need to worry about is not worrying."

Hailey smiled. "Uh…okay."

"I'll take care of the rest." He smiled. "Trust me?"

Hailey nodded. She could definitely do that.

God, help me keep faith with this man.

Eric had more than shown his character since she'd known him. He wasn't like any of the other marshals, and she loved that about him. He was both strong and gentle. Tough, and yet caring toward Kerry. Trusting him would probably turn out to be the easiest thing she'd ever done.

Hailey didn't want to do anything to mess this up, so she would just have to trust God to lead her. That would be something new for her, too. But given the peace she felt wash over her now, knowing her heart was finally where it should be and not fiercely guarded, she figured it was a good thing.

For the first time, she was who she was supposed to be.

Eric traced his thumb across her cheekbone. Hailey put her hand on the back of his neck and pulled his lips to hers. Before they touched, she said, "I'm in love with you."

She felt his lips smile against hers, and he said, "That's good, because I'm in love with you, too."

EPILOGUE

Eighteen Months Later

Eric strapped on his vest and checked his weapon.

Parker strode into the room where the team was preparing for the takedown of yet another escapee. "Ready to go?"

They filed out, their minds likely on the operation. Eric's would be, too, once he climbed in the SUV and they pulled away. But that would be in a minute.

He stopped by the desk next to his and squeezed Hailey's socked foot, stacked on the other atop the mass of papers and files she claimed were organized. Her shoes were likely discarded somewhere under the table. Who was going to fish them out for her if he was on an operation?

He crouched and retrieved her shoes so she'd be able to reach them later. "What time are you heading out?"

She looked up from her tablet and glanced at the clock. "About a half an hour." Her lips curled easily into the smile she gave him every morning at breakfast. His ring was on her finger, and he wore the gold band she'd slid on his that day at sunset eight months ago in her dad's backyard. "Sorry I'm going to miss movie night."

"Don't sweat it. That just means Kerry and I can watch

a rom com and you won't be huffing and sighing and pretending you're really fine with it when we know you're not." She grinned.

Eric smiled back. "I've gotta go."

Even if he'd rather spend the evening with his wife and daughter, that was the job. A job he'd come to love in the drama of the flood that happened the year before. Since then he'd fallen not only for his girls, but also for the town and the rush of fugitive apprehension.

Hailey slid her legs to the floor so her husband could help her to her feet. She'd finally quit wearing shirts that disguised her condition. She'd probably have tried to keep it private until the baby came, except for the fact they'd had to tell Jonah. Their job wasn't one where you could continue active duty when you were pregnant.

Months ago she would have been mad the team was heading out on an operation without her. But that was then. Now she had higher priorities. The first of many— she hoped—children that were hers and Eric's was growing inside her. Still, he'd thoroughly convinced her that Kerry was the daughter of his heart.

As much as Hailey loathed being stuck behind a desk, she was as excited for the baby to come as he was. The fact that he brought her double-chocolate cupcakes didn't hurt either. Then there was Kerry, who had held in the secret like a champion until they gave her the go-ahead to tell people. Now their daughter told every single person she met that she was going to have a baby sister or brother. She'd even started suggesting names.

Hailey pulled Eric close for a lingering kiss. He was going to be late, but she knew he didn't really care. The hall erupted into whoops and whistles. One day the rest of the team would get used to the married couple in the office, but apparently that wasn't going to be today. Half of them were married now, too, though that didn't seem to be a valid point to them.

Hailey leaned back and smiled up at her husband. "Take care."

Eric kissed her one more time. "Always."

* * * * *

Dear Reader,

Thank you for joining me on this adventure. Phew, I'm glad it turned out okay! I'm sure you are, too. There were some close calls for Hailey and Eric, but God brought them through the tough times. Doesn't He, though?

I'm grateful every day for the fact I've never gone through anything truly trying. My heart goes out to those who struggle constantly with the hard things in life. They are in my prayers. But God is faithful, and I love that He never changes. His love is constant, no matter how far from Him we wander.

To find out more about my books, you can go to www. authorlisaphillips.com or you can always email me at lisaphillipsbks@gmail.com. If you're not online, you can write to me c/o Love Inspired Books, 233 Broadway, Suite 1001, New York, NY 10279.

I would love to hear from you.

God bless you richly,
Lisa Phillips

REQUEST YOUR FREE BOOKS!
2 FREE RIVETING INSPIRATIONAL NOVELS
PLUS 2 FREE MYSTERY GIFTS

Love Inspired.
SUSPENSE

LIS13R

Love the Love Inspired book you just read?

Your opinion matters.

Review this book on your favorite book site, review site, blog or your own social media properties and share your opinion with other readers!

Be sure to connect with us at:
Harlequin.com/Newsletters
Twitter.com/LoveInspiredBks
Facebook.com/LoveInspiredBooks